Sprinkle with Murder

Jenn McKinlay

BERKLEY PRIME CRIME, NEW YORK

THE BERKLEY PUBLISHING GROUP
Published by the Penguin Group
Penguin Group (USA) Inc.
375 Hudson Street, New York, New York 10014, USA

Penguin Group (Canada), 90 Eglinton Avenue East, Suite 700, Toronto, Ontario M4P 2Y3, Canada
(a division of Pearson Penguin Canada Inc.)
Penguin Books Ltd., 80 Strand, London WC2R 0RL, England
Penguin Group Ireland, 25 St. Stephen's Green, Dublin 2, Ireland (a division of Penguin Books Ltd.)
Penguin Group (Australia), 250 Camberwell Road, Camberwell, Victoria 3124, Australia
(a division of Pearson Australia Group Pty. Ltd.)
Penguin Books India Pvt. Ltd., 11 Community Centre, Panchsheel Park, New Delhi—110 017, India
Penguin Group (NZ), 67 Apollo Drive, Rosedale, North Shore 0632, New Zealand
(a division of Pearson New Zealand Ltd.)
Penguin Books (South Africa) (Pty.) Ltd., 24 Sturdee Avenue, Rosebank, Johannesburg 2196,
South Africa

Penguin Books Ltd., Registered Offices: 80 Strand, London WC2R 0RL, England

This is a work of fiction. Names, characters, places, and incidents either are the product of the author's imagination or are used fictitiously, and any resemblance to actual persons, living or dead, business establishments, events, or locales is entirely coincidental. The publisher does not have any control over and does not assume any responsibility for author or third-party websites or their content.

PUBLISHER'S NOTE: The recipes contained in this book are to be followed exactly as written. The publisher is not responsible for your specific health or allergy needs that may require medical supervision. The publisher is not responsible for any adverse reactions to the recipes contained in this book.

SPRINKLE WITH MURDER

A Berkley Prime Crime Book / published by arrangement with the author

PRINTING HISTORY
Berkley Prime Crime mass-market edition / March 2010

Copyright © 2010 by Jennifer McKinlay Orf.
Excerpt from *Buttercream Bump Off* by Jenn McKinlay copyright © by Jennifer McKinlay Orf.
Cover illustration by Jeff Fitz-Maurice.
Cover design by Lesley Worrell.
Interior text design by Laura K. Corless.

All rights reserved.
No part of this book may be reproduced, scanned, or distributed in any printed or electronic form without permission. Please do not participate in or encourage piracy of copyrighted materials in violation of the author's rights. Purchase only authorized editions.
For information, address: The Berkley Publishing Group,
a division of Penguin Group (USA) Inc.,
375 Hudson Street, New York, New York 10014.

ISBN: 978-0-425-23342-9

BERKLEY® PRIME CRIME
Berkley Prime Crime Books are published by The Berkley Publishing Group,
a division of Penguin Group (USA) Inc.,
375 Hudson Street, New York, New York 10014.
BERKLEY® PRIME CRIME and the PRIME CRIME logo are trademarks of Penguin Group (USA) Inc.

PRINTED IN THE UNITED STATES OF AMERICA

10 9

If you purchased this book without a cover, you should be aware that this book is stolen property. It was reported as "unsold and destroyed" to the publisher, and neither the author nor the publisher has received any payment for this "stripped book."

For my mom, Susan Norris McKinlay,
I love you more than cupcakes!

Acknowledgments

People often ask where I get my ideas. Usually, I shrug because I have no idea. But with *Sprinkle with Murder*, I have to say, it was a little more in my face. In the course of one week, I listened as a soon-to-be married coworker agonized over what flavor cupcakes to have in her wedding cake tower, then my agent's partner blogged about how she checked out the local cupcake bakery in every city to which she traveled, and finally, a dear friend stopped by my house to tell me that a cupcake bakery had opened nearby and that they sold shots of frosting. It was the rule of threes and just like that I knew I had to set a mystery series in a cupcake bakery. So, I give thanks to Tara Dietz, Jessica Faust, and Sheila Levine for making my muse hungry for cupcakes.

Thanks must be given to my agent, Jacky Sach, for her skill and enthusiasm. Truly, you're the best. More thanks to my editors Allison Brandau to start and Kate Seaver to finish, with loads of help along the way from Katherine Pelz and Megan Swartz.

I'd also like to give a nod to my writing pals, the Ladies of the Loop, my fellow blog pals at the Mystery Lover's Kitchen, and for daily inspiration the gals at the blog Cupcakes Take the Cake. Locally, I must acknowledge Lulu's Cupcakes for being so gracious in answering my questions, giving me a tour of the kitchen, and for having the best chocoschnitzel cupcake ever.

I must thank my readers, Susan McKinlay, Susie Matazzoni, Jan Buckwalter, and Tom Gemberling for their always spot-on input. Also, I need to send hugs to my extended family, the McKinlays and the Orfs, who have patiently encouraged me through the highs and lows of a writer's life. And finally, first in my heart but last on the page, I want to give crusher hugs to my dudes, Wyatt, Beckett, and Chris Hansen Orf, you three are the frosting on my cupcake. I love you!

One

"Does she really think we don't see her?" Angie De-Laura asked her best friend and business partner Melanie Cooper.

Mel blew her blonde bangs off of her forehead and came around the counter of the cupcake display case to glance out the front window with Angie.

"How many times has she driven by today?" she asked.

"Seven times since we opened this morning, and twelve yesterday."

"You'd think if she was so worried about our shop stealing her customers, she'd be slaving away in her kitchen baking something."

"You'd think," Angie agreed.

Just then the icing pink, refrigerated van did another slow drive by their window. Angie and Mel smiled and waved. Olivia Puckett, the driver of the van and owner of a nearby bakery called Confections, gave them a wide-eyed stare and stomped on the gas, bumping the curb with one of the van's tires in her haste to get away.

"Maybe she'll get a flat," Angie said.

"We can always hope," Mel agreed.

Mel turned around. She refused to let Olivia Puckett's paranoia dampen her joy with her own shop. Fairy Tale Cupcakes had been a dream of Mel's for several years, and now it was finally open.

She loved everything about this petite shop nestled in the heart of Old Town Scottsdale. With a western wear store next door and a tattoo parlor on the corner, Mel felt as if she fit right in with the amalgam of quirky shops that filled this quaint neighborhood.

She had chosen a retro fifties décor. Everything was in shades of pink and gray with lots of chrome and glass.

Her main investor and childhood friend, Tate Harper, had made her tone down the pink a few notches; he said it made him feel constipated. Whatever.

Angie was refilling the silver napkin holders on the booth tables in front of the window, and she glanced frequently at the street to see if Olivia made another pass. Angie had been Mel's best friend for twenty-two years, since the first day of sixth grade when they met in homeroom.

Students were seated alphabetically, so she and Mel ended up next to each other. Mel had a powerful sweet tooth and frequently kept a stash of candy on her person. On that day, she had a milk chocolate bar, the kind without nuts.

Unfortunately, her sweet tooth caused Mel to be on the chubby side, which made her the object of much teasing. Wanting to be nice to the new girl, however, she offered Angie half of her candy bar. Angie looked so grateful that Mel knew she'd found a kindred candy freak. But when she reached across the aisle to hand Angie the chocolate, the class bully, Jeff Stanton, snatched it out of her hand with a mean laugh and said, "Thanks, Fatso."

Mel probably would have shed some private tears in the girls' bathroom, but Angie had exploded out of her seat and grabbed the candy out of Jeff's hand before he could shove it into his mouth.

"Who are you calling 'Fatso'?" she asked, and she poked him in the belly. Hard.

Jeff looked like he was going to slug her, but just then Joe DeLaura strode into the room. He was tall and muscular, and he was swinging his car keys around his index finger as if he hadn't quite gotten used to the fact that they were his. Or maybe he was just showing off. Either way, he frowned at Jeff and reached around him to hand Angie a paper lunch bag.

"You forgot your lunch in my car, Ange," he said.

"Thanks, Joe." She was still glaring at Jeff.

"Need any backup?" Joe asked, glaring at Jeff, too. Jeff visibly shrank on the spot.

"Nope," she said as Jeff scuttled back towards his desk.

"I'll pick you up after school."

Angie quickly leaned over to Mel. "You want to come over to my house today?"

"Sure," Mel agreed.

"And . . . hey, what's your name?" Angie asked.

"Melanie."

"And my friend Melanie, too," Angie called after Joe.

He glanced at Mel and shrugged. "Sure. See you."

It had marked the beginning of a perfect friendship. Then and now, Angie reminded Mel of a firecracker. Mel never knew when Angie was going to explode, and when she did, it was usually a sight to behold. Angela Marie De-Laura was short, with a curvy figure and long, wavy brown hair that reached halfway down her back. Her large, chocolate brown eyes were sharp with intelligence and warm with humor. She had a smile that lit up her whole face, and she frequently used it to charm her way out of anything she didn't like doing.

Having grown up tall and lanky, Mel had no curves to brag about. And now that she spent so much time in the kitchen, baking cupcakes, she kept her pale blonde hair cropped short in the back and long on top, giving her a thick set of bangs to keep from appearing too boyish. With her pale hair, pale skin, and blue-green eyes, Mel knew she and Angie were complete opposites, but maybe that's why they were such good friends. They balanced each other.

The bells on the door jangled, and Mel put on her greet-the-customer face. As soon as she recognized the tall man bearing two big boxes, however, her smile dimmed.

"Oh, it's you."

"Gee, it's great to see you, too," Tate Harper said. He put the boxes on one of the small café tables and stretched the kinks out of his back.

He was wearing his work clothes: a white dress shirt and charcoal gray slacks. His red power tie was askew, but Mel was pretty sure she could check her lipstick in the shine of his shoes.

Tate Harper, her other longtime friend, was handsome in a prep school raised with gobs of money, never had a worry in his life sort of way. But Mel had known him through a voice change, pimples, and braces. He would always be the big brother she'd never known she wanted until he strolled into her life at the age of eleven, quoting Groucho Marx and making her laugh so hard in study hall that she got detention for a week.

"I'm sorry," Mel said. "I thought you were a customer."

"Hunh." Tate gave a dramatic sigh and ran a hand through his wavy brown hair. "You know, 'It's better to be looked over than overlooked.'"

"Save it, Mae West," Mel chided him, and he grinned.

They had been trading classic movie lines since the day he had caused her to get detention. A few months later Angie made their duo a trio, and for the next seven years, the three of them whiled away most of their weekends watching old movies and eating junk food in the mini movie theater Tate's parents had in their house.

"Well, at least I got a smile out of Angie," Tate said.

"Be serious," Angie said from her spot in the booth by the window. "I'm laughing *at* you."

"Where's the love?" Tate spread his arms wide. "I sacrifice my lunch hour to come over here and help, and what do I get? No love."

Both Angie and Mel stepped forward and gave him quick hugs. He looked somewhat mollified.

"I just picked these up from the printer," he said. He opened the box on top and pulled out several bright pink flyers advertising the bakery's weekly specials. "I've got a connection at the local paper, and he says we can get these inserted in Sunday's edition."

"Excellent work, partner." Mel gave him a high five.

"That should make Olivia keel over on the spot," Angie said. "I'd love to see her face when she opens her paper, and there we are."

"Is she still staking out the shop?" Tate asked.

"Yes," Angie and Mel answered together.

"Maybe we should go and talk to her," Tate said. "I mean, we're only making cupcakes; she's got the whole cookie, cake, and brownie market to herself."

"Oh, I'll talk to her all right." Angie waved her fist. "I'll give her five good reasons to buzz off."

Mel and Tate exchanged a worried look. It was hard to say whether Angie would actually punch out Olivia, since things like that had been known to happen in the past. In fact, when they were in high school, one of the mean girls had spread rumors about Tate's sexual orientation because he refused to take her out. Angie had subsequently spent her foreign language lab sitting behind the same girl, carefully cutting a big chunk of the girl's hair off. With her headphones on, the girl had never heard her, and left the lab looking like a badly shorn poodle. As a general rule, it was never wise to mess with Angie or anyone she cared about.

"Maybe we should just give her a week or two to calm down," Mel said.

"That sounds like a good plan," Tate said quickly. He looked relieved. "Besides, you're going to be too busy over the next few weeks to waste any time confronting Olivia."

"I am?" Mel asked.

"Yes." Tate grinned. "Christie and I talked about it last night, and we agreed that you should be the one to bake our wedding cupcakes."

Angie dropped a napkin holder onto the black-and-white tile floor.

"Damn," she muttered as she scooped it up and examined it. "I'm such a butterfingers. I'd better replace this one."

Mel watched Angie disappear into the back room with the dented napkin holder. Good thing they'd ordered a few extra.

"So, you and Christie are going with cupcakes?" she asked. She hoped her voice didn't sound as strained as it felt.

"Yeah, Christie was thinking of getting a couture cake to reflect her clothing design business, but I told her that was ridiculous, since I've invested in Fairy Tale Cupcakes. This will be a great showcase for the shop. We're inviting five hundred people."

"Five hundred?" Mel repeated. "Wow! I don't even know five hundred people."

"Don't worry, I insist upon paying full price."

"No, no," Mel refused. "You're a partner."

"I won't take no for an answer." Tate glanced at his watch. "I'd better run. I have a meeting with a client at two."

"'Bye, Ange," Tate yelled towards the back. There was no reply. "See ya, Mel. I'll have Christie stop in to go over the details."

"Sounds great," she lied.

Her heart sank as the door banged shut behind Tate. This was bad, very bad. Mostly, because she wanted to like his fiancée, she really did, but she just didn't.

Christie Stevens was about as vapid a person as Melanie had ever had the misfortune to meet. The first night she and Angie had joined Tate and Christie for dinner, Christie had spent the entire meal complaining about her manicure. At least five times she asked them if her nails looked like they were made of gold. Apparently, she'd told her manicurist to use Gold Fiction polish by Chanel. But at thirty dollars a bottle, she was wondering if her nail girl had ripped her off and used some cheap knockoff instead.

By the second course, Angie had excused herself to go to the bathroom at least three times, and Mel had decided there wasn't enough wine at the bar to get her through the longest dinner ever; she was debating stabbing herself with her salad fork to get out of it. But then, Christie got a call on her cell phone, which she talked on all the way through the main course and halfway through dessert.

When Tate first started dating her, Mel was sure it wouldn't last. But then, oh horror, in a few short weeks and much to her and Angie's shock, Tate and Christie got engaged.

Mel and Angie were flabbergasted. Neither of them had seen this coming. And if Mel was having a hard time with it, Angie, with her mercurial temper, couldn't even be in the same room with Christie for fear she would say something that would destroy her friendship with Tate forever. Truly, it was a nightmare.

Angie reappeared with a new napkin holder. "Is Tate gone?"

"Just left," Mel said. "He yelled good-bye."

They were silent for a moment, both staring at the door.

" 'Getting married has ruined a lot of good men,' " Angie observed.

"*Dodge City*, 1939, well said," Mel noted with a laugh.

"Nuts, I thought I could sneak that one by you." Angie snapped her fingers.

"Fat chance." Mel was an old-movie buff of the first order. It would take more than *Dodge City* to stump her.

She felt a sudden pang as she wondered if Tate would still be a part of their late-night movie viewings. She knew Christie could not possibly be interested, and she doubted she was going to let Tate continue to join them. She didn't want to think about how much she would miss him.

She told herself not to panic. The wedding was still a couple of months away. Maybe he would get struck by a lightning bolt and snap out of it. But somehow she doubted he'd get that lucky.

Two

Christie was late. Forty-five minutes late, to be exact. Mel glanced at her watch for the third time in five minutes. She supposed she could call Tate to find out where his fiancée was, but she hesitated. Somehow, it felt like tattling if she called to complain that Christie had blown her off. Then again, she could pretend to be concerned for Christie's welfare, but sadly, Mel didn't think she was a good enough actress to pull it off.

She would give her five more minutes and then she was closing the shop. If Tate asked her what happened, she would have to say Christie never showed up. Surely, he couldn't get mad at her for that.

Angie had left early. She said she had a dentist's appointment, but Mel suspected it was an excuse, a lame one, to get out of this meeting. Although she wouldn't put it past Angie to book a root canal just to duck having to deal with Christie. From what they'd already seen, Christie could be a tad high maintenance, and Mel would be a big fat liar if she said she wasn't dreading working with her.

The bells on the door jangled just as Mel was beginning to think she'd been given a stay of execution. No such
luck.

Christie strolled in, wearing a cinched, thigh-length
leopard tee over white leggings and silver ballet flats. The
outfit screamed "Look at me!" She shoved her oversized
sunglasses onto her head, pushing her blonde extensions
back off her face.

"Oh, this is so cute!" she squealed as she glanced around
the shop. A tiny, furry head poked out of her oversized bag,
and Mel found herself staring at a dainty Yorkshire terrier
with a large purple bow on its head.

"This is Puddles," Christie said, and she put the dog on
the floor.

"Puddles?" Mel asked.

"Isn't she adorable?" Christie squealed again. "I was
going to name her Princess, but she piddles when she's
overexcited."

"How's she feeling now?" Mel asked.

"I don't know." Christie blinked at her, and then she giggled with a hand over her mouth. "Oh, you're being funny.
Tatums said you were funny."

Tatums? Mel felt her gag reflex kick in.

"So, what do you have to show me?" Christie asked.

Mel led the way to a small, round café table in the corner. On it, she had put an album of all of the weddings she
had done since she finished studying at the Scottsdale Culinary Institute several years ago. Primarily, she had done
cupcake tiers, but there were a few cakes as well.

"This should give you some ideas. Of course, we'll tai-
lor it to the style, colors, and flavors of your choosing."

"No," Christie said as she examined the first page. She
continued to flip through the book, saying, "No. No. No."

It seemed every page was a no. Mel could feel the back
of her neck getting hot. She forced herself to breathe in

through her nose, hold it, and let it out through her mouth. She did this several times. It didn't help.

Christie slammed the book shut with a final "No."

"Maybe you could tell me what you have in mind," Mel suggested. She was pleased that her teeth weren't gritted so tight that she could actually get the words out.

"I'm so glad you asked." Christie dug into her voluminous purse and pulled out a thick wad of paper. "Here's what I was thinking."

She took a deep breath.

"I want laser-cut cupcake liners in my wedding colors. I'm thinking our monogram should be worked into a delicate filigree, don't you agree?"

Mel nodded.

"We're inviting five hundred guests, so I need to have at least five different flavors of cupcakes."

Mel nodded again. So far this was doable.

"Of course we'll have a smaller wedding cake to sit on top of the cupcake tier for Tatums and I to cut together."

"Of course," Mel agreed. So far this was pretty standard. Mel felt a flicker of hope. "What are your wedding colors?"

"Red, white, and black," Christie said. "*Très élégant.*"

Mel nodded. Again, doable.

"So, what do you think?" Christie asked.

"It sounds fabulous," Mel said. "The popular flavors of wedding cupcakes are generally red velvet, chocolate, vanilla-almond, champagne, cookies and cream . . ."

"No." Christie wrinkled her tiny, upturned nose. "I can't have any flavors that have ever been used before."

"Excuse me?" Mel was quite positive she must have heard her wrong.

"I am Christie Stevens. I have a reputation as a cutting-edge designer in fashion. I can't have just any old cupcakes. I need originality. I need to be unique."

"So you want me to create five flavors of cupcakes that have never been created before?" Mel asked.

Christie clapped her hands together. "Oh, yay, you understand."

Mel was speechless. She glanced at the dog that was now sniffing at the display case and looking suspiciously like she was about to squat.

"And I just need you to sign this agreement," Christie said.

"Agreement?"

"Well, yes, it's just a tiny little legal formality." She unfolded the ten-page document in her hand and placed it on the table. "It simply states that the cupcakes you design for the wedding are owned by Tate and me, and can't be replicated in your shop or for any other persons—just us."

"You're joking?"

Christie pressed her lips together and glanced off to the side as if considering the question, then she looked back at Mel with hard blue eyes. "No."

"But that means you would own what I create."

"Well, Tatums did say we were paying you, although I can't imagine why, since he's your boss," Christie said. "And since we're paying you, I think we should own what we pay for, don't you?"

"Tate is not my boss," Mel said. "He's my partner."

"Without whom this cute little shop wouldn't exist," Christie sneered. She rose from her chair, and Mel got the distinct impression that she was being dismissed.

"Let me know when you have some samples for me to taste. Will Friday do?"

It was Wednesday. Mel felt her temples contract. This had to be a bad dream; surely she would wake up at any moment.

"Puddles!" Christie said, and stomped her foot. "You naughty little girl."

Mel glanced over and saw a rather large puddle for such a small dog seep across the black-and-white floor.

Christie's phone rang, and she fished it out of her bag while plopping Puddles back into the bag.

"Hello," she answered. "What do you mean the shipment is delayed? Well, I have a meeting with a buyer tomorrow. I need that shipment, Phoebe. Well, what are you going to do to make it right?"

Christie walked towards the door as she talked. She turned and gave Mel a dismissive wave as she stepped through the door and back onto the street. Unbelievable!

Mel glanced from the puddle to the door and back again. She'd just left. Her dog peed on the floor, and she just left. Mel wasn't positive, but she was pretty sure she felt an aneurysm coming on.

She grabbed a wad of paper towels and a bottle of Lysol, and cleaned up the mess. Then she called Angie.

"How was the dentist?" she asked.

"Uh . . . painful," Angie said. "My hygienist really enjoys her work, especially the gum scraping. How was your meeting?"

"We're going to have to kidnap Tate. I'm thinking if we drag him to Peru and leave him with no ID or money, it'll take him so long to work his way back that he'll miss his own wedding."

There was a beat of silence on the phone.

"So, it went well?" Angie asked.

Mel told her about the contract and the puddle. It took five minutes of spluttering before Angie calmed down.

"You need to take that contract to my brother Joe and have him look at it," she said. "He'll be able to tell you if it's legal or not."

"Looks pretty legit to me," Mel said as she flipped through the long sheets of fine print.

"Oh please, you think a pinky swear is a binding contract."

"It isn't?"

"Hey, as long as you don't say 'no crosses count' and then cross your fingers behind your back while making the pinky swear, you've got a loophole."

"I never say 'no crosses count.'"

"I know." Angie sighed.

"You're sneaky," Mel said.

"It's a part of my charm," Angie agreed. "I'm going to call Joe and see if he can drop by the shop."

"Do you really think that's necessary?"

"Oh yeah," Angie said. "I'll call you later."

Mel hung up. Joe DeLaura was going to stop by her shop. She felt the same fluttery feeling she always got when Joe's name was mentioned. She'd had this reaction to him ever since she'd seen him twirling his keys when they were kids. She thought she'd outgrown it, but judging by the skittery feeling she had at the thought of seeing him again, she hadn't.

Three

"Rise and shine," a lovely, lilting voice sang out from the kitchenette. "It's time to make the donuts, or in your case, the cupcakes."

Mel glanced at the blue digital clock on her nightstand. It read six thirty. A glance at the window shades, and she knew it was still dark out.

"Mom," she mumbled, but it was muffled by the pillow she pulled over her head. She tried again, "Mom!"

"Yes, dear?" Her mother appeared by her bed, bearing a cup of coffee. She put it on the nightstand and hunkered down beside the bed to be eye level with Mel.

"Why are you here?" Mel asked. She didn't mean to sound ungrateful—truly, coffee delivered bedside was like a small miracle—but when it came via her mother, Joyce Cooper, questions needed answers.

"We're taking your about-to-expire cupcakes to Waste Not Want Not," her mother reminded her. Joyce was big on not wasting food. Mel still remembered all of the starving children in China who would have killed for her broccoli. Unfortunately, her mother had never let her mail them any.

Now every Thursday was cupcake roundup. Joyce collected all of the cupcakes that were too old to sell in the shop and took them to her feed-the-hungry group.

"But even if it wasn't cupcake collection day, can't a mom just pop in on her daughter?" she asked.

Mel pushed the pillow aside. She took a bracing sip of steaming coffee.

"What if I'd had company?" she asked.

Her mother laughed. It didn't help that it was a full-on belly laugh. Surely, the idea of her having a date hadn't slid into the realm of the improbable and ridiculous.

"You're so funny," her mother said. Okay, apparently, it had.

Joyce Cooper flitted around Mel's kitchenette as efficiently as if it were her own. It could be, considering how much time she spent here, Mel thought sourly. But then she felt guilty. Joyce had been widowed ten years before, and Mel's only sibling, her brother Charlie, lived in Flagstaff with his wife and kids, and although they came to Scottsdale quite often, it wasn't enough to keep Joyce from smothering Mel.

Melanie couldn't help but wonder how her life would have played out if her father hadn't had a massive coronary and shuffled off to the great steak house in the sky. Charlie Cooper had loved his meat red, his beer stein full, and his cigar pungent, or smelly, depending upon whom you asked. He had always been the first guest at the party and the last one to leave. There was not a day in Mel's life that he hadn't made her laugh, and she couldn't help but wonder if this was why her mother had never dated again. No one had the same spark as Charlie Cooper.

It was this respect for her mother's grief, her understanding of it, that kept Mel from demanding her key back, even on the day she discovered that her mother had painted her bathroom mango orange. Joyce had promised it would make her look younger when she looked in the mirror. Instead, she felt as if she were an orange headed for the juicer. Still, she hadn't had the heart to repaint.

"So, I heard from Shelby Grady, at the grocery store, that Tate and Christie have asked you to make their wedding cupcakes," Joyce said.

"That's correct." Mel pulled herself up to a half slouch.

"Honey, do you really think that's wise?" her mother asked.

Mel glanced up and saw her own blue-green eyes staring back at her from her mother's face. There were more layers of wrinkles around them, but still, they were the same eyes she looked at in the mirror every morning. This was why she had never been able to lie to her mother. It would be like lying to herself, and what did that ever get anyone?

"Actually, from a business standpoint, it's very wise," she said. "They're inviting five hundred people to that shindig."

"But your poor heart," her mother said, putting a hand over her own chest. "How can you bear to see the man you love marry another?"

Mel flopped back down onto the bed. "Mom, we've been over this and over this. I am not now, nor have I ever been, in love with Tate. He's my friend. That's it."

"De Nile isn't just a river in Egypt, you know," Joyce retorted.

Mel groaned. Her mother had believed that she and Tate were meant to be together since the first day Mel dragged him home. Never mind that neither he nor Mel felt this way, Joyce had clung to the vision of her daughter as Mrs. Tate Harper since she was eleven, and she was not giving it up until they were both married to someone else, and even then she might not give it up. Joyce Cooper had staying power.

"Speaking of Tate," Joyce said, "we'd better get moving. He's meeting us downstairs in half an hour."

Mel sat up. "Why?"

Joyce blinked innocently. "I asked him for help, that's why."

"Help with what?"

"Carrying the cupcakes"

"There are maybe five dozen cupcakes," Mel said. "Surely, you and I can manage."

"I have a twinge in my back," Joyce said. "I didn't want to risk any heavy lifting."

Mel stared at her hard.

"Mom, is this another ploy of yours to push Tate and me together?"

"Now why would you ask a thing like that?"

"Because two weeks ago, you locked us in the walk-in cooler in the bakery, and we almost froze to death because you thought a near-death experience might bring us to our senses about our feelings for each other. Or does that little episode not ring a bell?"

"I should have left you in for five more minutes."

"Mom!" Mel was dismayed to hear her voice come out in a five-syllable whine. But truly, enough was enough. She rose from her bed and faced her mother. "You have to get a grip. Tate is marrying someone else."

"Aha!" Joyce pointed at Mel's face. "I saw that!"

"Saw what?" Mel looked behind her to see if there was a big spider or something.

"I saw your face when you said he was marrying some-one else," Joyce said. "It was not a good face."

"Oh, that." Mel sighed. "I'm trying to like his fiancée, I really am, but . . ."

"You can't, because you love him yourself."

"No, I can't, because she's a head case bridezilla, and I have no idea what he sees in her."

"Same thing," Joyce said. She opened the front page of the morning paper as if the discussion were closed.

"No, it isn't," Mel corrected her. "Now I'm going to take a shower, and while I'm in there, you're going to call Tate and tell him he doesn't have to come over and help with the cupcakes."

Her mother did not look up from the paper.

"I know you can hear me. Call him, Mom."

Her mother snapped the paper shut with a sigh and reached for the phone. "Fine," she said.

Mel shuffled to the bathroom. Joyce was going to have to go stay with Charlie in Flagstaff during Tate's wedding. Otherwise, Mel was afraid she might make a scene, especially during that "Does anyone have any objections?" part. Then again, it might be the only thing that saved Tate from making the biggest mistake of his life. She'd have to weigh public humiliation against saving her friend. Tough call. She'd have to think on it.

Mel was in the kitchen in the back of the bakery, prepping for their happy-hour baking class. Ten students were registered for the four-week session that featured drink-flavored cupcakes. Each student would bake and then decorate a dozen cupcakes to take home. Tonight's were pina colada. A pineapple cupcake with coconut buttercream icing, sprinkled with shredded coconut and topped off with a cherry and a pineapple chunk held in place by a paper umbrella. It was one of Mel's favorites.

Angie was manning the front counter. Mel glanced

through the doorway to see that it was under control. A group of older ladies sat in one booth, enjoying two cupcakes each, and a mom with two boys sat in another. One of the boys had chocolate frosting covering his face from chin to hairline and ear to ear. The other one had flipped his cupcake over and was eating just the cake. The mom was watching them with a small smile, as if trying to memorize this moment.

Mel turned back to the kitchen, feeling oddly fulfilled, as if in a very tiny way she had helped to make a memory. It felt almost as good as that first bite of a freshly frosted cupcake.

She was working at the large steel worktable in the kitchen, decorating her own batch of pina colada cupcakes to show the class what theirs would look like when they were finished. Mel used an open star decorating tip on her frosting bag and, holding it at a ninety-degree angle about a quarter of an inch from the top of the cupcake, she piped a spiral of icing, beginning at the outer edge and working inward. She then sprinkled some shredded coconut on top while the frosting was fresh, so the coconut would adhere to it.

While she worked, Mel's thoughts turned back to Christie and the wedding. After she had packed up Joyce and her about-to-expire cupcakes that morning, she had spent the day racking her brain, trying to come up with cupcake flavors that had never been done before. Christie wanted her to have samples ready tomorrow. Mel had a few new ideas she'd been planning to try, but if she made them for Christie and Tate's wedding after signing that contract, she'd never get to make them again. And what if they were really good?

She wondered if she should call Christie and put her off for a week or two or fifty. How could she possibly sign over her own creations? She supposed she could ask Tate to get her out of the contract part, but she'd seen Christie's ice-hard blue eyes.

She had a feeling Christie had never heard the word "no" in her life, and she doubted it would go well for the person who tried it. Also, this was a huge opportunity to showcase the shop, and if Christie threw a snit, she might not let Mel do the wedding. And what if she booked Olivia Puckett instead? Around and around Mel's thought whirled, with no resolution.

She was so lost in thought, it was a moment before she realized that someone was standing in the doorway, watching her. She glanced up, and there stood Joe DeLaura. She jumped, squeezing the icing bag too hard. A glob of coconut buttercream landed on the worktable with a *splat*.

He smiled. It was the same slow smile she remembered from when they were kids, and it still made the blood rush to her head. She was suddenly overly aware of her pink bib apron with the stylized, glittery script Fairy Tale Cupcakes across the front, the state of her messy kitchen, and the gobs of frosting that spattered the work surface, which included her. What must he be thinking?

Mel tried to shake it off. She was thirty-four years old now, and a successful small business owner. It didn't matter what he thought. She no longer had a crush on Joe DeLaura.

"Hi, Mel," Joe said. He pushed off from the doorway and walked towards her. "It's been a long time."

He was wearing a dark suit with a crisp white dress shirt and a blue tie. A faint pattern of triangles was worked into the tie, giving it texture. He was clean shaven and his straight black hair was cut short, almost military short. He was taller than she remembered, and she had to look up to meet his gaze. His brown eyes, so like his sister's, moved over her in return.

"You look different than I remember," he said.

"I'm not fat anymore."

He looked taken aback, and Mel could have bitten her tongue in half. *Good one, remind him that you were a lard butt as a kid.*

He took in her distress and smiled again. Then he said, "I don't remember you as fat. I remember you as the girl who giggled a lot."

"Giggled?" Mel asked, appalled. "I think I'd rather you remembered me as fat."

This time he full-on grinned at her, and Mel thought she might faint. Okay, so maybe she wasn't completely over her crush.

"It was a very charming giggle," Joe reassured her.

"Yes, well . . ." Mel forced herself to stop looking at him. She was obviously incapable of forming a complete sentence when he was in her field of vision. It was best to avoid direct eye contact.

"Angie told me you were stopping by to look over the wedding contract," she said. She arranged the last of the finished cupcakes on a platter and pushed it towards the center of the worktable. "Thank you for taking the time."

"No problem," he said. "I've been meaning to check out the shop. It's just been chaos at the DA's office. This gave me a nice excuse to get out of there on time for a change. I like what you've done with the place. It's . . . homey."

"Thanks." Mel wondered if homey was a euphemism for messy. "Let me just go get the paperwork for you."

Her office was a small room off of the kitchen. She had left the contract on top of her desk, so she ducked in there to grab it, wiping her hands on her apron as she went.

"I don't really know if there's anything you can tell me," she said. "The contract seems pretty straightforward."

Joe was sitting on one of the stools that surrounded the table. He held out his hand, and she gave him the paperwork. While he scanned the pages, she wiped down the tabletop. He let out a couple of "hunhs," and she wondered what that meant in legal speak.

After a few minutes, he looked up and dropped the papers onto the table with a sigh. "You're right, it's pretty clear. She wants exclusive ownership of whatever you create for her wedding."

"No loopholes?"

"Not a one," Joe said. "It seems very controlling, even in these days of overlitigation."

"I thought so, too." Mel sighed. She had known it was unlikely, but she had sort of hoped she could sign the contract and not have to give up her creations. "What do I owe you for your time?"

"Like I would charge my sister's best friend and business partner. You can't be serious."

"I'm not." Mel grinned. "But good manners demanded that I offer."

Joe returned her smile. He looked so out of place sitting next to her pink KitchenAid mixer in his severe-looking suit. It was almost comical.

He continued to regard her steadily. "You know, the brothers are really unhappy that Ange gave up teaching to open this shop with you."

"Yeah, I know," she said.

Mel braced herself for what she knew was coming: another DeLaura lecture. Angie had seven older brothers who spent their lives trying to manage hers. It was undoubtedly the reason she was still single. Every man she brought home got chased away by the disapproving scowls of her brothers. If she didn't love them all so much, Mel was sure Angie would have moved to Australia by now

"They . . . uh . . . we were wrong," Joe said. Mel knew she looked surprised when he smiled. "She's happier working with you than she has been in a long time. And really, all we want is for her to be happy."

"I know," Mel said. "I want the same thing."

They were quiet as a moment of understanding passed between them. In all the years Mel had known Joe, she didn't think they'd exchanged as many words as they had in the past twenty minutes. So maybe she was over her schoolgirl crush.

"Well, what's a guy got to do to get a cupcake around here?" he asked, breaking the silence.

"Oh, yes, of course. I'm sorry, I should have offered you one earlier. What's your poison?"

"What do you recommend?"

"I love them all." Mel laughed and pushed her bangs off her forehead. "But I'm partial to the blonde bombshell."

Joe raised his eyebrows, and his gaze swept her from head to toe. Mel felt her cheeks grow hot. Oh, dear, he didn't think, surely he couldn't think, that it was named for her.

"I was thinking of Marilyn Monroe when I came up with that one," she mumbled. "It's an almond-flavored cake topped with vanilla buttercream and toasted almonds."

"Sounds good to me."

Mel nodded, feeling like an idiot. What was it about Joe DeLaura that flatlined her brain?

"I'll be right back," she said. She trotted out front and loaded up a plate with a cupcake and grabbed a napkin, a fork, and an ice-cold glass of milk. She returned and plunked down the cupcake in front of Joe.

She took the contract and returned it to her office so it wouldn't get lost in the hullabaloo of that night's class.

When Mel turned around, Joe had plunged his fork into the cupcake and taken a bite. The look that spread across his face could only be described as sublime, and Mel felt her confidence rush back. If there was one thing she knew she did well, it was baking cupcakes.

"This is the most amazing thing I've ever tasted in my life," Joe said, looking at her in wonder.

Mel felt her face get hot again, but this time it was with a flush of pleasure. She sat across from him while he finished the cupcake. When he scraped the plate with his fork, she wondered if she should offer him another, but he rose and carried his plate and fork to one of the three industrial sinks. He even rinsed them. Bravo, Mama DeLaura.

"For that, I feel like I should have been more help to you," he said.

She shrugged. "I appreciate the confirmation that it's as binding as I thought."

"You should talk to Tate," Joe said. "I can't imagine he knows what she's asking. He doesn't strike me as the type who would want you to give up your own creations like that, especially when it goes against his interests as part owner in this business."

"I suppose."

"And you're not going to take a word of my advice, are you?"

"Probably not," she admitted ruefully.

He walked back to stand beside the chair where she still sat. Mel had to crane her neck to look up at him.

"I know what's different about you." His hand brushed across the back of her head. "You cut your hair. It suits you. It makes your eyes look enormous."

"Thanks," Mel said. Her throat felt oddly constricted, and her voice was gruff. She coughed.

"Thank you for the cupcake," he returned. He headed through the door back into the shop, calling out, "See you."

Mel raised her hand in a small wave. As soon as he disappeared, she ran into her office. On the back of the door hung a tiny mirror. She studied her reflection, trying to see what Joe had seen. Did her eyes look enormously pretty, or did she look like a big-eyed E.T. freak? But even E.T. was cute in his own way, right?

All she saw was Melanie Cooper, cupcake baker and inept flirt. She turned away with disgust. She hadn't seen Joe DeLaura in years. There was no reason to suppose she'd see him anytime again soon. Or so she thought.

Four

Mel decided against Joe's advice (and Angie's) and signed the contract. Partly because she didn't want to let Tate down, and also because she couldn't ignore the reality that the business would get a real shot in the arm from the wedding publicity. And there would be a lot of publicity as two of Scottsdale's wealthiest residents tied the knot.

The next morning Mel was running on less than no sleep. She had spent the night baking cupcakes, mixing frostings, and rolling out fondant. After innumerable attempts, she had finally crafted five new cupcakes in a wide variety of flavors and in Christie's colors of red, white, and black. As far as she knew, they'd never been created before. Could anyone else have come up with a dark chocolate cupcake with cherry filling and a dark chocolate ganache topping sprinkled with dried cherries? That was only one of the five, but it was her favorite.

She called Christie's cell phone as soon as the shop opened, and left a message that the cupcakes were done.

She didn't hear back from Christie all day.

As it grew later and later, Mel found her temper going from irked to annoyed to really ticked. Cupcakes dried out quickly, and she wanted Christie to taste hers while they were still fresh. The urge to tear up the contract was becoming almost too strong to ignore. She left two more messages for Christie and finally called Tate.

"Harper Investments, Tate Harper speaking," he answered.

" 'Yes, but, I don't like to say so, sir, at this moment, sir, but everybody knows you're crazy,' " Mel said.

"Hey! *Bringing Up Baby*." Tate cited the quote with obvious pleasure. "Is that what's showing tonight?"

"Yep. I need a dose of Cary Grant and Katharine Hepburn. Ange and I will be over to your place about nine."

Mel was standing at the front counter, using their pink phone. At the mention of her name, Angie glanced over from where she was dusting a display rack full of cupcake kitsch and nodded, confirming her attendance at movie night.

"Sounds great. Christie has some fashion shoot thing in her studio, so she's busy until late. We might even be able to do a double feature."

"Sweet," Mel said. "About Christie, I called to let her know the cupcake samples she wanted are ready, but I haven't heard from her. Could you make sure she gets the message?"

"Absolutely," Tate said. "I really appreciate you doing this for us, Mel. I sort of feel like I've been hit by a truck with all this wedding stuff. Having your cupcakes there will make it seem more friendly. Does that make sense?"

Mel was quiet for a second. Was this her opportunity to ask him if this wedding was what he really wanted? Could she ask him that?

"Oh, I have another call coming in," he said. "See you at nine."

" 'Bye, Tate." Mel hung up. Damn! The moment was

lost to her indecision. Maybe tonight, during the movie, she'd have another chance to broach the subject.

The door swung open, distracting Mel from her thoughts as a middle-aged, portly man strode in with his younger, skinnier sidekick on his heels. As always, she was struck by how much Uncle Stan looked just like her dad: same jowls and thinning hairline, same girth and bowlegged gate.

"Uncle Stan!" she cried as she dashed around the counter to be enfolded in the same comforting bear hug she'd been getting from him ever since she was a child.

Angie darted up for her own hug, and they both smiled at Detective Rayburn, Uncle Stan's latest trainee.

"What'll it be today, boys?" Angie asked. "We have fresh Red Velvets or a nice Cookies and Cream."

Uncle Stan licked his lips in anticipation. "A Red Velvet for me."

"Nothing for me," Rayburn said. He patted his flat belly, as if to reassure himself that he couldn't gain weight by just standing in the bakery.

Angie shook her head and gave Mel a look that said you just couldn't trust someone who didn't eat cupcakes. Privately, Mel agreed. But since he was Uncle Stan's partner, she endeavored to be nice to him.

"How's business?" Uncle Stan asked.

"Booming," Mel said. "I think we're really getting a following."

"Did you look into that security system we talked about?"

"Yep," Mel said. She looked. She didn't buy it, because it was too expensive, but she did look.

The bakery phone rang, and Mel excused herself to pick it up.

"Fairy Tale Cupcakes, this is Mel. How may I help you?"

"You can stop calling my fiancé to complain about me." It was Christie, and she sounded annoyed.

"Excuse me?" Mel said.

"I do not need you calling my fiancé to tell him I'm ignoring you," she snapped. "When, in fact, I've just sent two of my girls over to your little shop to pick up the cupcakes."

"I can assure you I said no such thing," Mel said. She set her teeth to keep from saying more.

Angie glanced at her from where she was wiping down the counter. Her eyes were wide, letting Mel know that her tone had been uncharacteristically sharp; both Uncle Stan and Detective Rayburn were watching her as well.

"Look, I have a real business with real problems to deal with. Someone will be by to pick up the damn cupcakes. In the future, I would appreciate it if you would call me, and not Tate."

"Check your cell phone," Mel said. "I did call—repeatedly."

"I don't think I like your tone," Christie said. "I don't care how long you've been friends with Tate. I'm the one who's marrying him. It's not my fault you couldn't close the deal all of these years you've been palling around with him."

"What?" Mel choked.

"You heard me." Christie's voice was a low hiss. "I know both you and your little friend have been trying to bag Tate for years. Well, you couldn't, and I did. Deal with it."

Christie hung up on her, and Mel felt her temper surge and explode.

"Uh!" she grunted. She went to put the phone back in its cradle, but her hand missed and the phone slipped onto the counter, which made her temper flare again. She smashed the phone against its holder three times, and shouted, "I hate her! I hate her! I hate her! I hope she chokes on those cupcakes."

Uncle Stan and Detective Rayburn stood frozen. Uncle Stan's mouth was wide open with Red Velvet cupcake hanging out. He quickly shut his mouth and swallowed.

"What was that about?" he asked.

Mel crossed her arms on the counter and put her head down. Her temper tantrum had taken the last of her energy.

"I'm sorry," she said. "No sleep will do that to a girl. *That* was the bridezilla my friend Tate is marrying. She is a selfish, narcissistic nightmare. I've tried to like her, truly, but I just can't."

Detective Rayburn's cell phone rang, and he turned away to take the call.

"Tate has always seemed like a reasonable young man," Uncle Stan said. "Maybe he'll see the light before he says 'I do.' "

"Maybe," Angie and Mel said together, but neither one believed it.

"Stan, we've got to go," Rayburn annouced.

Uncle Stan shoved the last of his cupcake in his mouth and waved as he hustled out the door.

"She was that awful?" Angie asked.

Mel was about to recount the conversation when the bells on the front door jangled and two young women walked in. One was a willowy, dark-haired, dark-eyed girl with skin so pale it almost glowed. The other was tan, blonde, and decked out in sparkles from head to toe.

"We're here to pick up an order of cupcakes," the blonde one said. She wiggled as she walked, unfortunately reminding Mel of Christie's dog Puddles. The other one, the scary-looking one, seemed to glide across the room.

"I just love this place, don't you, Alma?" the giggly one asked her companion. "It's just so cuuuuuute."

"That's what we were going for," Angie said dryly. "Cuuuuuute."

The one called Alma just glared. She radiated a feeling of doom, and Mel and Angie exchanged a look. If anyone was in need of a cupcake, it was this girl.

"What are your names?" Angie asked.

"Why do you need our names?" the one called Alma asked, looking irritated.

"Your order would be under your name," Angie said.

"Oh, they're not for us, silly," the blonde girl said.

"As if," Alma added. Her tone made it clear that there'd be snowball fights in hell before there was a box of cupcakes with her name on it.

"What name would the order be under then?" Angie asked. Mel could tell she was about out of patience, and she joined Angie behind the counter to give her backup.

"Christie Stevens," the blonde said proudly. "Only the most brilliant designer ever."

"She sent you, then?" Mel asked.

"Obviously." Alma said each syllable slowly, as if she thought the word was too big for Mel to comprehend.

Mel saw Angie's fingers flex and she feared that she might smack the girl with a spatula, so she quickly intervened. "Angie, they're in a box in the walk-in. Would you get them for me, please?"

"Gladly." Angie glared at the dark-haired girl and stomped into the back room.

Mel studied the gothic-looking young woman. She was dressed head to toe in black, wore too much makeup, and somehow managed to suck all of the joy out of the air around her, as if she were a mini black hole.

The blonde one, however, was as bright as a buttercup and obviously worshipped her boss. Mel had noticed that not only did the blonde dress like her, but she also had some of Christie's mannerisms down. She covered her mouth when she giggled, and the giggle sounded just like Christie's. Eep!

"So, you're Christie's assistants?" she asked.

Alma glared at her from behind a thick curtain of black bangs. "Hardly. We're designers."

"Really?" Mel asked. "That must be fascinating."

"Oh, it is," the blonde said on a breath. "And working for Christie is such an honor. Why, she's just totally all that, you know?"

"Shut up, Phoebe," Alma snapped.

"Hmm," Mel grunted noncommittally.

Alma glanced around the room as if the cheerful pink walls were making her physically ill. She glided over to a corner booth and sank down as if just being in the shop was making her weak.

"I'll need you to sign for the cupcakes," Mel said to Phoebe.

"Sure," she said, with a shrug she tossed her blonde hair over her shoulder.

Mel quickly rang up a receipt and handed it and a pen to the girl. She scrawled her name just as Angie returned with a pink box with gray and black retro starburst symbols on it.

She offered the box to Alma, who looked as if she'd rather die than be seen carrying such a thing.

"Don't you have a bag you could put that in?" she asked.

Angie glowered at her and found a plain white bag under the counter. She put the box in the bag and handed it to Alma.

"Have a lovely evening," Angie said with so much syrupy cheerfulness even Mary Poppins would have gagged. Mel had to turn away to keep from laughing.

The bells jangled as the door shut behind the girls.

"Someone quick call the Addams family and tell them Wednesday is on the loose," Angie said.

"She was positively creepy, wasn't she?"

"And what was with Malibu Barbie?" Angie asked. "A girl could strain something looking that happy all the time."

"Hard to say who I'd rather be stuck in an elevator with, that's for sure," Mel said.

"Oh, not me," Angie retorted. "I'd take old gloom-and-doom. Probably at night she can transform into a bat and fly; much better chance of a rescue that way."

"Let's just hope Christie loves those cupcakes, so we don't have to do this again." Mel glanced at her watch. "We'd better beat feet if we're going to get to Tate's in time."

"I'm bringing the popcorn."

"I've got Jujubes and Raisinets," Mel said. "And Tate promised to make coffee milk shakes."

"We'd better enjoy this," Angie observed. "If Christie has her way, this may be our last movie night together."

"Tate will always make time for us," Mel said.

She was lying, and they both knew it. Christie was a force to be reckoned with, and if she pulled the plug on movie night, Mel knew there wasn't much Tate or anyone else would be able to do about it. She didn't say as much to Angie, but judging by her conversation with the bride-to-be on the phone, Christie had a warped view of their friendship and would be doing her level best to end it.

\'\'\'\

Mel resided over the cupcake bakery in a studio apartment, Angie rented a duplex in the neighborhood that surrounded Old Town Scottsdale, and Tate lived in a luxury penthouse condominium on the canal just north of Old Town.

Needless to say, movie night was always at Tate's pad,

just as it had been his house when they were growing up. He had the spectacular view of the city, the Italian marble bathrooms, the guest suites, the fully stocked steel-and-granite kitchen, and, most important, the media room, with leather recliners, a sixty-inch, flat-screen plasma HDTV, and a Bose home theater system. Life was good if you were a Harper.

They didn't have assigned seating for movie night, but they all sat in the same spot every week anyway. Mel sat in the recliner to the left while Angie and Tate shared the sofa, each end reclined, with one empty seat in between them. Mel wondered if Christie would soon be filling that seat. Somehow she doubted it.

Exhausted from baking cupcakes all night, Mel knew Tate's upcoming wedding was more on her mind than usual. Well, that and getting reamed by bridezilla sort of made it hard to ignore.

While Kate Hepburn quipped with Cary Grant, Mel glanced over at Angie and Tate. Angie was tucked under a cashmere throw, as the October evening had grown chilly. Tate was sprawled in his recliner with a bucket of popcorn on his left and the remote on his right.

She watched the reflection of the black-and-white film flicker across her friends' faces and felt a sharp pang in her chest. Was this one of the last nights they'd all be together? Would Christie forbid movie night? Could Mel accept her as Tate's wife, or would their friendship slowly suffocate under Christie's overbearing presence until it ceased to be? Mel felt a wave of deep depression wash over her. She knew she was overtired and it was a very bad time to be thinking about anything, but still she was besieged by a foreboding she couldn't seem to shake off.

Abruptly, the theme music from James Bond filled the room.

"What the . . . ?" Angie sat up, annoyed, while Tate

paused the film with one hand and fumbled in his pants pocket with the other to retrieve his cell phone.

"Sorry," he said. "I forgot to shut it off."

Angie gave him an eye roll while he checked to see who it was. He frowned.

"It's Christie," he said. "I have to take it. Sorry."

As he stepped out of the room under the paused and watchful faces of Kate and Cary, Angie gave Mel a dark look. It said louder than words that Christie was already ruining their movie night. Mel sighed.

"What do you think she wants?" Angie asked.

"Not a clue," Mel answered. She was afraid Christie was calling to complain about the cupcakes, but she didn't want to go there.

"Let's find out." Angie threw the blanket aside and stood up.

"But that's eavesdropping," Mel said as she followed Angie out of the room.

They scuttled down the hall in their socks, following the sound of Tate's voice. His home was done in rich earth tones that complemented the toffee-colored tile that ran throughout. Angie led the way, past the guest rooms and the large home office, to the master suite. The French doors were open, and Tate was standing on the balcony on the far side of the immense room. The brilliant lights of the Valley of the Sun rolled out before him like a carpet of stars.

Mel seldom thought of how wealthy Tate really was, but every now and then it crept up and slapped her in the face, and she marveled that the three of them had been friends for all these years despite their divergent backgrounds.

He shifted his feet, and Angie grabbed Mel's arm and yanked her to the floor behind the king-sized bed in the center of the room.

They crept under the bed—no dust bunnies there—and

out the other side, where they hugged the wall until they were close enough to hear his side of the conversation.

"Yes, I know," he said. There was a lengthy pause. "I know you wanted me there tonight, but it's movie night."

There was another lengthy pause, and Mel was pretty sure she could hear the sound of a high-pitched nag on the other end of the line.

"Christie, they've been my best friends since I was a kid," he began, and was obviously interrupted. "Why is that weird?" Pause. "So what if they're women? They're my friends."

Mel and Angie exchanged a look. Tate had dated girls before who hadn't liked that his two best pals were women. He had a group of guy friends he played golf and hoops with, but when he wanted to relax, he kicked around with the two of them.

Mel supposed it was because, just like when they were kids, Tate could be himself with them. His father, a scarily stern man, had kept Tate on a pretty tight leash, grooming him to take over Harper Investments. It was Tate's mother who had encouraged his friendship with Mel and Angie, as if she knew that Tate needed them to keep him from turning into a replica of his cold, withdrawn father.

"Christie, don't ask me to choose between you and my friends, because you won't like how it turns out." Tate's voice was harsh, and Angie looked at Mel with raised eyebrows. Tate seldom lost his cool.

The wail that Christie let out was loud enough for Mel to hear from several feet away. Tate winced and held his phone away from his ear.

"I'm sorry, Christie," he said, sounding sincere. "I didn't mean that. That was terrible of me to say."

He paused, and Mel could hear a series of high-pitched shrieks coming out of his phone.

"No, of course, I won't call off the wedding," he said.

"Yes, I know I proposed, and I meant it. You are the most important person in my life. You're my best friend."

Angie made a guttural gagging sound. Tate turned at the noise, and both women ducked behind a wing chair, hoping he didn't catch them. Mel peeked around the back of the chair. Tate was facing the view and speaking in a low tone, obviously still trying to soothe the bride-to-be.

Mel pushed Angie back under the high bed, and they scrambled to the door and down the hall. Angie pushed open the bathroom door and yanked Mel inside with her.

She shut and locked the door, and turned the water on, before she turned to Mel with a scowl.

Mel sat on the vanity seat while Angie paced back and forth in front of the long counter with double sinks. "We're supposed to be his best friends."

"I know, but things change," Mel said.

"She's muscling him into this marriage. He can't be in love with her."

"He's marrying her. He must care about her on some level."

Mel reached over and shut off the tap. She doubted Tate would be able to hear them through the thick walnut door.

"That's because he's Tate, and Tate always does what he says he'll do," Angie said. "It's a character flaw."

Mel smiled. It was true. Tate had always been as good as his word, and up until now that had been a good thing.

A sharp knock on the door sounded, and they both started.

"Hey, you two, hurry up," Tate called.

"On our way," Mel replied as Angie ran the sink again.

When they opened the door, Tate stood there, staring at them, and Mel feared he knew they'd listened in on his conversation. An apology was halfway out of her mouth when he shook his head and asked, "What is it about women and going to the bathroom together?"

"Buddy system," Angie said as she strolled by to resume her seat on the couch. "If you fall in too deep, it's always good to have someone to pull you out."

Tate gave her a quizzical look, but shrugged and flopped back onto his side of the sofa. As the movie resumed, Mel crunched her popcorn, but even with extra movie theater butter it tasted like paste.

Tate didn't mention Christie's call until Angie and Mel had donned their hooded sweatshirts and were headed out the door. Tate's was one of four penthouses, and his front door opened into a large lobby decorated with real ferns, more Italian marble, and mirrors that made you look skinny. The doors to the other luxury homes were closed, and Mel wondered if the owners were home.

"Uh, Mel, I need to talk to you," he said.

Mel and Angie turned around to look at him as they pushed the elevator button for Down.

"You might as well say it in front of me," Angie said. "Because she's just going to tell me on the ride down anyway."

Tate grinned and said, "It's not a secret."

"Oh," Angie said, looking disappointed.

"No, Christie just wants Mel to stop by her studio tomorrow morning," he said. "She tried the cupcakes you made, and she has some suggestions."

"Oh," Mel said. "What time?"

"She has a meeting at eight. She was wondering if you could stop by at seven thirty."

"In the morning?"

"Sorry, I know you're not a morning person. Do you want me to give you a wake-up call?"

"No, I'll be fine." Mel knew she sounded sulky. She tried to shake it off. Tate had enough on his plate. He certainly didn't need her being less than supportive, so she added, "I'll be happy to."

"Thanks, Mel," he said. "You're a pal."

The three friends hugged, and as the elevator door shut on Tate waving good-bye to them, Mel couldn't help but think he looked more like a lost little boy than one of the country's smartest investment analysts.

Five

There was a bite to the brisk morning air. Mel pulled her jacket closer, loving the fact that after a summer where the mercury had hovered around 115 degrees for weeks, it was now down into the sixties in the early morning, and it actually felt cold.

Christie's design shop was located near Scottsdale's premier shopping center, Scottsdale Fashion Square, just north of Old Town. This was Christie's home office, but she had another shop in Los Angeles, where she sold to an even more exclusive clientele. Her specialty was clothing for the ultra-pampered rich woman in her late twenties and early thirties who maintained a size zero capped with a surgically enhanced bust line; in other words, her specialty was herself.

Mel parked her red Mini Cooper, which she'd bought because it had the same last name as her, in the narrow lot in front of the shop and hurried across the sidewalk to the front door. Nestled between an interior design firm and a day spa, Christie's studio was very mod, with floor-to-

ceiling glass windows framed in brushed steel and doors
to match.

Mel leaned close to the glass to peer in. Bright lime
green and iridescent purple puffy chairs were the accent
colors set against a background of stark white. Clear ca-
bles mounted in the ceiling supported steel racks of clothing, making it look as if the clothes were floating. No more
than ten items were on any rack, and Mel would bet the
point spread that there wasn't anything over a size four
on display. Her inner chubby adolescent bristled at the
thought.

It had been years since anyone had called her Fatso, and
looking at her tall, thin reflection now it was hard to rec-
oncile the lithe, muscled woman she had become with the
plump kid she'd been, but still the scars ran deep.

Melanie had been a large Marge all the way through
school, and at college when others gained the freshmen
ten, she had gained the freshmen thirty. She had gone to
UCLA; Tate was off to Princeton; and Angie had attended
Northern Arizona University.

If growing up in Scottsdale and being chubby had been
tough, in LA it had been a soul crusher. So Mel dieted and
exercised and starved herself until every ounce of baby fat
had been eradicated.

It had been the worst four years of her life. Missing
Angie and Tate and their late-night movies, Mel had
thrown herself into her studies and graduated at the top
of her class with a degree in marketing. She had been a
whiz-bang young exec working for a firm in LA when
she realized the only happy moment of her day was her
drop-by at her neighborhood bakery to get her daily
sweets fix.

She immediately quit her job, packed a bag, came home
to Arizona, and enrolled in the Scottsdale Culinary Institute to be a pastry chef. After she graduated, she topped off

her studies by spending several weeks in France, studying at the Paris Lenotre School to learn the *tours de main* from a professional French pastry chef, the sort of things she couldn't learn from a book. But an interesting thing happened to her while in France.

Mel learned to love food again. Not the unhealthy "I hate myself so I'm going to eat five burgers" love; instead, she noticed that the women in France had a healthy relationship with food and she wanted that, too. The French ate better food; they used all five senses, and they lingered over their food in a love affair that was joyous, not destructive or guilt-ridden. It changed Mel's relationship with food, and when she returned home, she felt like a butterfly coming out of her cocoon.

She was no longer the rail-thin coed with food issues. Instead, she was a lean but slightly curved version of her old self who loved good food, loved running her own cupcake bakery, and finally, after years of struggle, felt good about herself.

That is, until she looked at the skimpy outfits hanging in Christie's shop; then the worm of self-doubt wriggled in her belly like a parasite that fed on self-loathing. Mel closed her eyes. No. She was not going to let someone else's warped idea of what a woman should look like poison her own acceptance and appreciation of herself.

Shaking herself like a wet dog, Mel knocked on the glass door to let Christie know she was there. She glanced at her watch. It was seven thirty-five, so she was essentially on time. She waited, turning to see if anyone else was open, but no, it was too early for the other shops.

She glanced through the glass again, wondering if Christie had heard her. She didn't see any movement. She knocked again, louder this time. Still no answer.

Maybe Christie was in back and couldn't hear her. Mel walked around the row of stores. Behind the building, there were three doors. Christie's gold Porsche was parked in front of the middle one.

Mel rapped on the steel door with her knuckles. It made a hollow sound that echoed in the early morning quiet. She frowned. Christie's car was here. Where was she?

She turned the doorknob. To her surprise, it opened. She pulled, and let it swing wide. The back room was floor-to-ceiling rolls of fabrics in every hue imaginable. Mel walked into the room feeling much like Alice at the bottom of the rabbit hole.

"Christie?" she called. Silence greeted her.

She walked through the rows of fabrics until she came to another room full of sewing machines, drafting tables, and tailors' mannequins. Sketches of clothing on line drawings of exaggerated silhouettes littered the room. Mel stopped to study several of the sketches. The styles were very different. One was dark and sleek, and she guessed the work belonged to the grim Alma. The other was an explosion of bright colors. Phoebe's, perhaps? She noted that the initials CSD were scrawled in the lower right-hand corner of each sketch. It appeared she had marked each with the company initials CSD for Christie Stevens Designs. Interesting.

"Christie, it's Melanie," she called out. "I'm here to talk about your cupcakes."

Her footsteps echoed on the hard floor, and she supposed Christie must have just popped out. Should she stay? Should she wait outside? She couldn't help but be miffed. She wasn't a morning person to begin with, and here she was at—she checked her watch—seven forty and there was no sign of Christie. She wondered if she should call Tate, but given how that had gone over with Christie the last time, she thought not.

She left the large, industrial design room and entered the shop. It was empty. She supposed she should just plunk down in one of the puffy chairs and wait. She spied some high fashion magazines on a small table by the window. At least she'd have something to read while she waited.

She rounded a rack of skirts and froze. A leg, a very slim leg in black hose, wearing a Christian Louboutin platform pump with a bright red heel, was sticking out from under a hanging rack of evening gowns. Mel knew right away this was no mannequin that had toppled over.

She ran across the floor, ducking under the gowns. Sure enough, Christie was sprawled as if she'd fallen and had knocked herself out. For a nanosecond, Mel was sure she'd tripped and banged her head. But her pasty coloring alerted Mel that something was wrong, very wrong.

"Christie, are you all right?" she asked. She put a hand on each side of Christie's face and patted her cheeks. She felt stiff to the touch, and Mel yanked her hands back.

Mel stared at Christie's chest, but there was no rise and fall. She put a finger on Christie's exposed wrist, hoping to find a pulse. A cupcake, covered in dark chocolate fondant, rolled out of Christie's curled fingers. Mel paid it no mind as she frantically felt for any sign of life. There was nothing. Christie was dead.

Mel refused to believe it. No, no, no. She raced to the service counter and grabbed the receiver to the phone. She punched in 9-1-1.

"I need an ambulance right away," she said as soon as the dispatcher answered. "I'm at Christie Stevens Designs on North Scottsdale Road. She's not breathing, and I can't find a pulse."

The dispatcher deployed an emergency crew and stayed on the line with Mel, asking her questions. Yes, she was safe. No, there was no sign of a break-in. No, Christie wasn't responding. When the ambulance arrived, screeching into the parking lot with a squeal of wheels and siren blaring, Mel ran to the front door to undo the dead bolt and let them in. She stood huddled in a corner while the EMTs worked on Christie. They had no more luck reviving her than Mel.

Feeling numb, Mel pulled out her cell phone and called Tate.

" 'Good morning, Stella,' " he answered.

Oh no, a movie quote. Mel twisted her lips at the irony of his choice.

" 'Good morning, dream boy,' " she returned, her voice hoarse.

"Nice catch," Tate said. "I thought I might stump you with *The Killers*."

"Not likely," Mel said. She glanced over at the EMTs and saw one shake his head at the other. She turned away.

"So, how did it go? Do you girls have our wedding cupcakes all figured out?"

"Oh, Tate." Her voice broke and she sucked in a breath, trying to ease the lump in her throat.

"What? What is it, Mel?" He sounded alarmed. He knew her too well not to know that something was seriously wrong.

"It's Christie," she said. "It's bad."

"What? What is it?" His voice dropped to a cautious level as if a whisper could muffle any incoming bad news.

"When I got here this morning, she didn't answer the door, so I came around the back," Mel said. "And I found her . . . Tate, she's dead."

"I'll be right there." He disconnected.

Mel put her phone away but stayed in the corner. The EMTs were conferring with the police officer who had arrived on the scene just after them. No one moved Christie. No one touched the clothing rack above her. No one picked up the cupcake that had rolled out of her hand.

As if remembering she was there, the officer left the EMTs and made his way to her side.

"Miss?" he said.

"Cooper," she supplied. "Melanie Cooper."

"Miss Cooper, I'm Officer Reinhardt. I'm going to ask you to wait outside," he said. "A detective is on the way, and I'm sure he'll want to speak with you. In the meantime, we need to keep the integrity of the crime scene intact."

"Crime scene?" she asked.

The officer realized his mistake as soon as Mel repeated his words. "I can't verify that, ma'am, but I need you to vacate the area until the detectives arrive."

She wanted to question him, but as if he sensed this, Officer Reinhardt took her by the elbow and led her outside. Mel sat nearby on a concrete bench beneath an acacia tree. The morning had grown warmer, but still her skin felt chilled.

More cars arrived, one of which was the county medical examiner's van. Mel waited for Tate, wondering where he was, what he was thinking, and if he was going to be okay. Finally, his Lexus zipped into the parking lot. He had to park several spots away. Mel stood and waved at him. He ran to her side.

"What's going on?" he asked. His brown hair was mussed. Mel suspected he hadn't even run a comb through it, and his clothes were wrinkled as if he'd grabbed them off the floor in his haste.

"Oh, Tate," she said. She grabbed his hand and held it tightly in hers. "It's bad, very, very bad."

"Tell me . . ."

"Mel," a voice interrupted. Mel turned to see her uncle Stan striding toward her.

Uncle Stan had worked as a detective with the Scottsdale Police Department for as long as Mel could remember. He was one with his shield; in fact, she had never seen him without it or his gun. Mel didn't hesitate, she ran and hugged her uncle Stan as hard as she could.

"Hey, now," Uncle Stan said and patted her back. "What

are you doing here, Mel? I just got a call that a young woman was found dead."

Mel stepped back and looked into her uncle's kind face. "I know. I found her."

"Oh, Mel, are you okay?" he asked. "You look pale. You should be sitting down. What happened?"

"Wait," Mel said. She reached behind her and pulled Tate forward. "Uncle Stan, you remember my friend Tate Harper?"

"Of course. How are you doing, son?" he asked as the two men shook hands.

"Not too well," Tate said. "I'd like to go and see her."

"Uncle Stan," Mel said. "The young woman is Christie Stevens. She's Tate's fiancée."

Uncle Stan's gaze snapped to Tate. He seemed to study Tate for a moment before he said, "Let me find out what's going on. I'll be right back."

He hustled past them, and Mel watched as the glass and steel doors swallowed him up like an appetizer before the big meal.

"Tell me what happened," Tate said while they both watched the door for Uncle Stan's reappearance.

Mel told him everything she could remember.

"So there was no blood or marks or any indication that she'd been harmed?" Tate asked.

"None that I could see," Mel said. "It was like she was asleep, but she wasn't. I'm so sorry, Tate."

"Ahem." They turned to find Officer Reinhardt standing behind them. "The detectives would like to see you now."

"Oh, okay," Mel said. "Officer Reinhardt, this is Tate Harper. He's Ms. Stevens's fiancé."

Understanding passed over the officer's features, followed swiftly by a speculative glance that Mel did not like.

"If you'll follow me, please," he said as he led the way into the shop.

Mel squeezed Tate's hand once more for courage and followed. Uncle Stan and another detective stood at the back of the shop while several people wearing badges from the county medical examiner's office worked around Christie's body.

"Here they are," Officer Reinhardt said.

The detectives exchanged a look, and Uncle Stan stepped close to Mel.

"I need to ask you some questions," he said. "My colleague, Detective Rayburn, will escort you to your fiancée, Tate."

Tate nodded as he followed Detective Rayburn towards the cluster of medical personnel.

"Mel, tell me exactly how you came to be here this morning and what you found," Uncle Stan said.

"Certainly." She told him everything. About having a seven thirty meeting and how no one answered, so she tried the back door and found it unlocked, and finally how she saw Christie's leg, tried to revive her, and called 9-1-1.

Uncle Stan didn't interrupt. He took several notes and nodded while she spoke. Mel's voice cracked when she talked about realizing that Christie was dead, but she swallowed hard and forged on.

"What was your relationship with the victim?" he asked. Mel paused. She knew Uncle Stan already knew how much she disliked Christie; he'd been in the shop when she lost her temper and announced how much she loathed her. Since this was official police business, however, she skirted around the truth.

"I'm a longtime friend and business partner with her fiancé, Tate. She and I were just getting to know each other."

"So you wouldn't call her a friend?" he asked. She could tell by his narrowed gaze that he'd caught on that she was being vague.

"Not yet," Mel said. "I really haven't known her that long."

Uncle Stan gave her a hard stare, and Mel fought the urge to squirm. Why did he have to look so much like her dad? It made it impossible to hide anything from him.

She had done nothing wrong, and she certainly wasn't going to give him any reason to think that she had. Still, she couldn't help but notice that her hands were sweaty and her heart was thumping harder in her chest than normal.

"Cooper," one of the crime scene workers called, and both Mel and Stan answered.

"I think that's for me," Uncle Stan said with a small smile. The tense moment was broken.

"Stick around. I may have more questions for you. If you think of anything urgent, call my cell."

"Okay." Uncle Stan had been programmed into every phone she had ever owned. You never knew when you might need a family member on the force.

He escorted her back out the door and gave her a quick hug before he went to talk to the crime scene personnel.

The other detective was standing with Tate. Mel stood off to one side and waited. Tate looked as if someone had sucker punched him. He kept shaking his head as if trying to make it all go away. The detective handed him a card, and Mel went to stand beside him.

"How could this be?" he asked. His voice cracked with emotion, and Mel looped an arm around him. He was trembling. She patted his back, wishing she knew what to say.

After a moment, he pulled away. "I need to call Christie's parents."

Mel nodded, and watched as he drew out his Black-Berry. She sat back down on the concrete bench while he walked to the corner to make the call in private. She did not envy him this task.

"What's going on?" a voice asked just behind Mel.

She turned on the hard bench and saw Alma, the goth designer, standing behind her and smoking. Again, she was all in black from her spiked black hair to her scuffed black combat boots.

Mel wasn't sure what to say. Should she be the one to tell Christie's staff what had happened? She didn't think so. Phoebe, the blonde with the superbouncy personality, joined them. Her hair was up in a ponytail and held back by a wide headband. She was wearing cherry red leggings with a red and white zebra-striped top. She pushed her sunglasses up onto her head and studied the door to the studio, which someone had propped open with a brick.

"Hiya," she said, as chipper as a morning songbird. "Why are we out here?"

Mel glanced around for Uncle Stan. There was no sign of him.

"It seems . . . well . . ." she stammered, hoping someone would show up and rescue her from this task, but no one did. "It seems that Christie, well, she's dead."

Alma squinted at her through a plume of smoke. Mel could tell she thought she was messing with her.

Phoebe, on the other hand, laughed. "You're so funny. Seriously, what's going on? Did the fire alarm go off again?"

Just then Tate walked by with his phone pressed to his ear. He was pacing, as he did when he was agitated, and Mel heard him say, "The police don't know what's happened. My friend Melanie Cooper arrived to meet with Christie this morning, and that's when she found her. She was nonresponsive."

Alma and Phoebe looked at Mel with wide eyes and, seeing the confirmation of Tate's words on her face, Phoebe let loose with a scream that drew Mel's nerves as tight as a piano string before it snapped.

Several officers came running, one of whom caught

Phoebe as she fainted. Mel rose to help, but an EMT arrived and half carried, half dragged Phoebe to a nearby ambulance.

Alma slumped onto the concrete bench. "So, it's true, then? The wicked witch is dead?"

"I'm afraid so," Mel said. She was taken aback by the hostility in Alma's tone, but she said nothing.

"I don't suppose I should be surprised," Alma said, lighting another cigarette. "Someone was going to do the bitch in sooner or later. I guess I just thought it would be later."

Mel had not been a fan of Christie's, but she was stunned by the callousness in Alma's tone. What had Christie done to the young designer that she hated her so much?

She was about to ask when one of the EMTs came rushing back. "Excuse me, are you Alma?"

She turned towards him. "Yes?"

"Your friend is asking for you," he said.

"We're coworkers, not friends," she corrected him.

"Okay, your coworker is asking for you," he replied, looking irked. "Could you put that out and come with me, please?"

Alma took one more long drag before she crushed the cigarette under the hard rubber toe of her boot. She gave Mel a put-upon look before she followed the man in the blue uniform.

When Mel looked up, Tate was standing in front of her. He looked shattered. Without thinking about it, Mel put her arms around him and hugged him tight.

Six

A flash popped, and Mel looked over her shoulder and saw a photographer standing there. He was all aquiver like a dog with a juicy bone. It didn't take a genius to realize that because of Tate's fortune and Christie's quasi celebrity, this was going to be front-page news. Tate hugging another woman at the scene of his fiancée's death wasn't going to look good, no matter how you sliced it.

"Your name, miss?" the photographer asked.

"Oh, hell, no!" Tate snapped.

He shoved Mel behind him and took a step towards the guy like he was going to punch him, but Mel held on to his arm and forcibly pulled him back into the studio to wait for Christie's parents.

"Tate, don't," she said.

As they hovered near the wall on one side of the studio, Mel's phone began to ring. It was distinguishable by her *Gone With the Wind* ring tone. She scrambled to pull it out of her purse and checked the number. It was the cupcake shop, so she knew it was Angie.

"Hello," she said.

" 'I know the perfect way to kill someone. You clog their arteries with whipped cream, chocolate mousse, butter . . . they go like that!' "

"Angie, what are you saying?"

"I'm quoting *Manhattan Murder Mystery*. Don't tell me I got you with that one. I thought it would make you laugh. You must be about ready to wring bridezilla's neck by now."

"Oh, man, I thought . . . never mind," Mel said with a sigh. Tate looked at her with a frown. "Listen, something has happened over here at the studio."

"What?" Angie demanded.

"I don't know if I should say over the phone," Mel replied. She could see Uncle Stan and the other detective having a heated conversation with the coroner, and every once in a while the other detective glanced towards her and Tate. It didn't give her the warm fuzzies; in fact, she felt herself beginning to sweat.

"Oh, come on," Angie said. "You can't start to tell me and then stop. What's going on? Is Christie being a nightmare or what?"

"I'm going to wait outside for Christie's parents," Tate said. "They'll be here any minute."

"Okay."

"Okay, what?" Angie asked. "Are you going to tell me now?"

Mel slid down the wall towards the back of the shop, where she figured she could speak without being overheard. In a quiet voice, she said, "Angie, Christie's dead."

"What?" Angie shrieked.

It was loud enough that Mel had to move the phone away from her ear or risk blowing out her eardrum. Quietly, she described the events of the morning. Angie said nothing, and a few times Mel had to ask her if she was still there.

"How's Tate taking it?" Angie asked, her voice tight with worry.

"I think he's in shock. I don't know what to say to him."

"Do you want me to come over?" Angie asked.

Mel glanced around the room. She would love to have Angie with her to bolster her through this nightmare. But the medical examiner's people were swarming the building, and the police were in every inch they weren't. Spectators were beginning to gather outside, and several news vans filled the parking lot. No, Mel was going to leave as soon as Uncle Stan told her she could. There was nothing Angie could do but stand helplessly with her, and really, what was the point of that?

"Thanks," Mel said, "but I'll meet you at the shop as soon as I get done here. I'll text you if there's anything to report."

"Let me know if you change your mind," Angie said. "And give Tate a hug from me and tell him to call me if he needs me."

"I will," Mel promised, and closed her phone.

It seemed like days passed before Uncle Stan sent her on her way with a hug and a promise to call her later. She had told her story about finding Christie three times to him and the other detective, and watched in sympathetic horror when Christie's parents arrived.

Her father was short and pudgy, clad in pastel golf duds. He was still wearing his spikes, and they scratched against the floor like fingernails on a chalkboard. Her mother was rail thin and mature, but fighting the aging process for all she was worth. Wearing a beige Donna Karan wrap dress with a fat strand of pearls at her throat and diamond clusters at her ears, she looked as if she had just left a ladies' brunch. This was not the way they had planned to spend their day, to be sure.

When Christie was placed in a body bag and wheeled out to the van that would take her to the medical examiner's office, Mel felt her throat get tight as Christie's mother broke down and sobbed onto her husband's shoulder. He patted her with an awkward hand, his own eyes misty with unshed tears. Mel couldn't even imagine the depth of their pain. When she glanced at Tate, he looked as if he'd been run over by a truck.

Mel felt the same helplessness she'd felt when her father died. She'd watched her mother suffer and grieve, and had not known what to say or how to help. Now she was watching one of her closest friends go through the same thing, and again she didn't know what to do. Granted, she was not paralyzed by her own sense of loss this time, but still, she felt woefully inadequate to help Tate.

Then Christie's father glanced over at her. He studied her face as if memorizing it for a police lineup. His eyes narrowed and his nostrils flared, and Mel got the distinct impression that she would soon be hearing from Mr. Stevens. She doubted it would be to place an order for cupcakes.

\'.'.\'

When Mel arrived at Fairy Tale Cupcakes, the shop positively sparkled, and she knew Angie had channeled her worry into cleaning.

"How's Tate? What happened? How did she die? Should I bring him some soup or cupcakes?" Angie barraged Mel with questions.

Mel raised her hand to signal "Whoa!"

"Sorry, I've just been so worried." Angie twisted her pink apron in her hands.

"I think I need a Death by Chocolate, although that's an unfortunate name, given the circumstances," Mel said. She led the way back to the kitchen. In the walk-in, a huge tray of chocolate cupcakes sat waiting. Mel took two and went to sit at the worktable.

Angie sat across from her, and they silently unwrapped their decadent dark-chocolate-on-chocolate treats. Mel didn't bother with a plate or a fork.

"I know emotional eating is bad," she said. "But if not now, then when?"

Neither of them spoke until the cupcakes were gone.

"Tate's in shock," Mel said. "I don't know what happened. I don't know how Christie died. And I don't know if Tate would be up for cupcakes just yet. Maybe in a few days."

Angie nodded. Mel went on to recount the morning's events, and Angie listened. When Mel finally wound down, they sat silently together. Neither of them knew what to say.

The front door opened with a jingle of bells, and Angie jumped up to greet their customer, probably relieved to get away from the grim news. Mel wadded up their spent cupcake papers and tossed them into the stainless steel garbage can beside the table.

For a moment, she toyed with the idea of closing the shop, but then, what would she do? Go home and relive this morning in all its Technicolor glory? No. Instead, she pulled on her apron and followed Angie back into the shop.

After helping with the morning crush, she spent the next hour baking a fresh batch of strawberry cupcakes called Pretty in Pinks. Mel was inventorying the display case while Angie packed up an order for a customer, when she glanced up and saw Olivia Puckett's refrigerated van drive by.

"How many times has she driven by today?"

"That would be the eighth," Angie replied.

"That's it," Mel said. "I've had it."

"What are you going to do?" Angie asked. "You can't stop her from driving down the street."

"No, but maybe I can discourage her."

Angie raised her eyebrows as Mel hurried back to the

kitchen. Before Angie could stop her, Mel dashed back out
the front door with a bowl of the leftover buttercream frosting in one hand and a spatula in the other.

When Olivia's pink van circled back to crawl by the
shop again, Mel counted to three and scooped up a spatula
of pink frosting and let it fly. It landed with a deliciously
satisfying *splat* on Olivia's windshield.

Olivia stopped hard with a yelp of her brakes, and
hopped out of the van.

"What do you think you're doing?" she demanded.

"Oh, oops!" Mel said, completely unrepentant. "I was
just mixing, and I guess my frosting got away from me."

She lifted another spatula full and flicked it onto the
other side of the windshield.

"Hey, you did that on purpose!" Olivia accused.

"Did not."

"Did, too."

Olivia clocked in somewhere in her early fifties. Her
corkscrew gray hair was twisted into an untidy knot on top
of her head, and her sallow complexion was mottled with
ire. Mel was pretty sure that if Olivia had had something to
throw back at her, like a rock, she would have.

"Puckett, why don't you get a life and stay out of mine?"
Mel asked in her most scathing tone.

"Ha! I can't help it if I have so many deliveries in this
area," Olivia said. "What's the matter? Afraid I'm cutting
in on your business?"

"Really? Deliveries?" Mel scoffed. "You drive by fifteen times a day. I see more of you than my own mother,
and that's saying something."

Olivia huffed out a breath and swaggered towards Mel.
She stuck a meaty finger into the bowl of frosting and popped
it into her mouth. She wrinkled her nose in disgust.

"You call yourself a chef?" Olivia spat the frosting onto
the sidewalk. "That's disgusting."

Acutely aware of the crowd that was gathering, Mel did her best to look superior. "Coming from a woman who models her cupcakes after store-bought ones, I'd say that's high praise."

Olivia sucked in an indignant breath. "I do not!"

"Do t . . ." Mel's words were cut off when she was yanked back into the store by her apron strings.

"Have you lost your mind?" Angie demanded. Then she stuck her head out the door, and yelled, "Playtime is over. We just got an order for over two hundred cupcakes. Olivia, you might want to go back to Confections and bake something!"

Olivia gave Angie a bug-eyed look and scooted back into her van. She sped off with her windshield wipers flapping frosting in all directions.

Angie turned back to Mel. "Seriously, what were you thinking?"

Mel sagged, clutching her bowl of frosting to her chest. "I wasn't. I'm just not having a very good day. Did we really get that big of an order?"

"No, it was for four dozen," Angie admitted. "But hey, it got Olivia moving, didn't it?"

The front door jangled and several customers poured in, probably curious after the ruckus. Mel was grateful, not only for the business but also because, if she kept busy, then she could stop thinking about finding Christie dead. Or so she hoped.

✶ ✶ ✶

The post-lunch dessert crowd was gone, and Mel and Angie leaned wearily on the counter.

"If this keeps up, we're going to have to hire some help," Angie said. "I'm worn out."

"Five hundred cupcakes a day will do that," Mel agreed.

With its western-style, squared-off buildings with front porches that sported benches made out of wagon wheels, Old Town Scottsdale was a tourist mecca, and Mel had positioned her shop right in the heart of it. They got more walk-in traffic from tourists than they did from locals, although they did a solid business with them as well.

Now that it was late afternoon, it would be quiet until just after dinner. Mel left Angie to clean up the front while she headed into the back to restock the display cases.

She was deep in the walk-in when she heard a familiar lilting voice.

"Melanie?"

She stepped out of the walk-in, carrying an aluminum tray full of Tinkerbells. These were lemon cupcakes with raspberry buttercream frosting rolled in pink sugar. She resisted the urge to cram three in her mouth. Barely.

"Oh, baby," her mother wailed, and opened her arms wide.

Mel spun away and scooted the tray onto the large steel table in the center of the kitchen, before turning to receive her mother's hug.

"Are you okay, Mom?" she asked. She patted her mother's back, breathing in the familiar scent of her Estee Lauder perfume.

"Am *I* okay?" Joyce Cooper stepped back and grabbed Mel's shoulders. She peered at her face as if trying to see into her soul. "I think the question is are *you* okay?"

Ah, now it made sense. South Scottsdale might be in the middle of a metropolitan area of more than four million people, but it remained a small town at heart and gossip moved faster than a roadrunner chasing a horned toad. She suspected news of Christie's death had reached her mother, and the fact that she had been the one to find the body had not been far behind.

"I'm fine," Mel said. "A little freaked-out but fine."

Her mother continued to study her. A frown in the shape of a V formed between her eyebrows. She was clearly not satisfied with either "fine" or "freaked-out."

"Is there something you want to tell me?" she asked.

Mel leaned against the table. She'd heard this question before; when her hoard of candy was found under her bed as a kid, when she got a D- in algebra, and most memorably when her mother found her birth control pills in her laundry duffel on a weekend home from college.

Needless to say, Mel did not like this question, especially when it was topped by the concerned frown.

As always, she opted to play stupid. It had never worked before, but hey, there's a first time for everything.

"No," she said, drawing out the lone syllable. "Not that I can think of."

"I'll stand by you, you know," Joyce said, her voice fierce. "No matter what you've done."

"Excuse me?" Mel asked. "As far as I know, for the past few months I've done nothing but bake cupcakes."

"Really?" Joyce asked. Her voice was ripe with doubt.

Then it hit her. Her mother wasn't here about her finding Christie, she was here about her altercation with Olivia.

"Oh, now I get it," Mel said. "Yes, I did it. I'm not proud of it, but she's been bugging me for months. Frankly, she had it coming."

Joyce gasped and clapped her hands over her mouth. She looked horrified.

"What?" Mel asked.

"No remorse?" her mother asked. "Not even a little?"

Mel thought about it. "No, not really."

"Oh, no, where did I go wrong?" Joyce wailed. She paced back and forth around the kitchen. "It's because your father died, isn't it? Why couldn't he be here to deal with this? He'd know what to do."

She glanced at the ceiling. "Just you wait until I see you

again, Charlie Cooper. I'm going to get you for sticking me with this mess."

"Um, Mom, I think if I offer to pay for her van to be washed, all will be well," Mel said. "Not that I want to, but I will if you think it'll make it right."

"Her van?" Joyce gaped at her daughter.

"Yeah," Mel said. "I think that's more than generous, given how annoying she's been."

"The girl is dead. Why would she care if you pay to wash her car?"

They stared at each other, and Mel got a sinking feeling in her chest.

"Mom." It was Mel's turn to frown. "What, exactly, do you think I've done?"

Joyce glanced around the room, as if to make sure they were alone. "Whacked Christie Stevens, of course."

"WHAT?" Mel yelled. She didn't mean to, but truly, if her mother had said she'd been spawned by an alien abduction, she couldn't have been more shocked. "Are you kidding me?"

"Hush. It was a crime of passion. I'm sure we can make an excellent defense for that."

"You think I murdered Christie?" Mel asked. She plunked her hands on her hips and faced her mother down. "Have you lost your mind?"

"Well . . ."

"Don't you 'well' me," Mel said in a fine imitation of Joyce. "How could you, Mom? How could you think that of me?"

"Tate is the love of your life," she said. "It's understandable that the thought of him marrying another might provoke . . ."

"What? Homicidal tendencies?" Mel smacked a hand down on the table. It sounded like a shot, and made her mother jump. It was louder than Mel had intended, and defused her first surge of anger. However, she was still mightily annoyed. "Mom, I am not now, nor have I ever been, in love with Tate. He's my friend and that's it."

Joyce stepped close to her daughter and patted her hand. "That was excellent, I almost believed it. Don't you worry. We'll hire the best attorneys money can buy."

With a quick hug and kiss, Joyce left. Mel watched her go. Her powers of speech had left her, and she stared stupidly at the doorway, wondering what else the day could bring.

"What was that about?" Angie ducked her head in. "I heard you slap the table all the way out front."

"My mother thinks I whacked Christie Stevens."

"Did you?" Angie asked.

"What?" Mel asked, shocked. Surely, Angie couldn't think that, too.

"I'm just messing with you," Angie said with a grin.

Mel sagged with relief. "Not funny."

"Oh, I don't know. The look on your face was classic."

Mel scowled.

"Don't worry. You know your mom has always been deluded about you and Tate."

"Yeah," Mel said. "She doesn't understand that we're all just friends."

Angie moved across the table from Mel and helped her shift the Tinkerbells on the tray to make for easier access.

"So, you've never had feelings for Tate?" Angie asked.

Mel glanced up at her. "You're kidding, right?"

Angie looked momentarily uncomfortable, but she pressed on. "No, I'm serious. Has there ever been a time when you thought you might like to date him?"

"Date Tate?" Mel asked. "The guy who used to have me check his braces for stray lettuce leaves before social studies? The pal who totaled my first car when I was trying to teach him to drive a stick shift? The same buddy who sounded an air horn at my cooking school graduation? That Tate?"

Angie was laughing out loud by the time Mel was done.

"Sorry," she said through her chuckles. "I don't know what I was thinking."

"You've been hanging around my mother too much," Mel said. "Don't get me wrong. Tate's on the short list of people I'd give a kidney to, but he's not a romantic prospect—not now, not ever."

With the cupcakes all nicely arranged, Mel hefted the tray up to her shoulder and headed out the door to restock the display case.

"You must feel the same way," she said, but Angie was behind her and Mel missed whatever she said as she walked into the shop and found Uncle Stan and Detective Rayburn waiting for her. Uncle Stan did not look happy.

Seven

"Uncle Stan, it's not your usual day for a cupcake!" Angie hurried around the counter to give him a hug. He returned the hug and smiled down at her.

"Hi, Angie. Hey, how are the brothers?"

"Oh, you know, lovable, annoying, lovable, same old, same old," she said with a wave of her hand.

During their teen years, Uncle Stan had gotten to know several of Angie's seven brothers quite well for a variety of misdeeds and misdemeanors.

Mel slid the tray into the display case and glanced over the top. Uncle Stan was studying her.

"Mel, do you have a minute? I'm actually here on official business."

Angie looked over her shoulder at Mel with wide eyes.

"It's okay," Mel said.

Several of the customers at the booths and tables were watching the interaction, so Mel pasted a pleasant smile on her face. She didn't want anyone thinking she was failing a health inspection. She gestured for Uncle Stan and company to come around the counter to talk to her in the back.

"What can I do for you?" she asked.

She wasn't sure whether she should sit or stand. If she sat and they didn't, it would be intimidating, so she stood and leaned against the worktable, hoping to look casual as opposed to rude.

Rayburn jingled the change in his pocket, as if he were eager for something to happen. He made her nervous, and Mel studied him more closely than she had before. He was short and skinny with a cowlick and a prominent Adam's apple. He was a new recruit to the detective squad, and he looked it. Judging by the mustard stain on his tie, Mel was betting Rayburn was single and likely to remain that way. Looking at the two of them, she couldn't help being reminded of Laurel and Hardy. As much as she loved Uncle Stan, this did nothing to reassure her.

Rayburn met her gaze briefly before he carefully moved it over the room. She knew he was cataloging every detail of her kitchen. There was no reason for it, but it still made her nervous.

"What's going on, Uncle Stan?" she asked, turning her attention back to him because he seemed to be running the show.

"We have some more questions."

"All right," Mel replied.

Detective Rayburn walked around the kitchen. He peered into the empty bowl of her pink mixer, and Mel wondered if he was foraging for food. Maybe she should offer him a cupcake. Would that constitute bribery? Wait . . . what would she be bribing them for?

"Mel?" Uncle Stan interrupted her thoughts, and she suspected he'd said her name more than once.

"Yes?" She forced herself to focus on him.

"There was a box of cupcakes found in Ms. Stevens's

studio," he said. "The markings on the box indicate that they came from your shop. Do you have something you want to tell me?"

"Oh, God, you talked to Mom, didn't you?" she asked.

"I'm concerned about you," Uncle Stan said.

"Did she tell you that I'm in love with Tate?" Mel asked. "Uncle Stan, do not believe her."

Rayburn paused in his search of the kitchen to listen to their conversation.

Uncle Stan raised one bushy eyebrow, which encouraged Mel to continue. "Mom has had it in her head that I've loved Tate since we were kids. I don't, I never have, I never will."

She watched as Uncle Stan seemed to relax just the littlest bit at this news.

"So you were at her shop to go over the flavors of cupcakes you'd baked?" he asked.

"Yes," Mel said, feeling relief that someone was finally listening to her.

"Did you bring them over this morning?"

"No, two of her employees came by and picked them up yesterday."

"Which employees?"

"Two young women named Alma and Phoebe."

Uncle Stan's eyebrows moved again, and she'd have bet her secret for moist cupcakes (use oil, not butter) that he was thinking about Alma's surly attitude. He made a note in his pad.

"What were some of the flavors?" Rayburn asked.

Mel felt him walk behind her, and she glanced over her shoulder; he was examining the area around her triple-basin steel sink. She knew it was unreasonable, but she was not liking him very much.

"There were five different kinds, a chocolate cupcake with cherry filling, a lemon coconut . . . um . . . can I ask why you're interested in this?"

Uncle Stan opened his mouth to answer when he was interrupted by a voice at the door.

"He probably wants the recipe. He's the only detective I know who relaxes by watching the Food Network."

Mel spun around. Joe DeLaura was standing in the doorway. His dark blue suit fit him perfectly and added to his aura of authority. Detective Rayburn straightened up at the sight of him.

"What can I say? Kitchen wizardry runs in the family," Uncle Stan said as he reached out to shake Joe's extended hand.

"Oh, please, I've tasted your meat loaf. It's only good for use as a doorstop," Joe said.

Uncle Stan looked put out and Mel laughed, feeling the tension in the room evaporate.

Uncle Stan adjusted his belt around his middle as he said, "Need I remind you who invited the new fire chief over to his house for a barbecue and then lit his backyard on fire?"

To Mel's surprise, Joe laughed out loud, and she was momentarily distracted by how handsome he was. His laugh was deep, and she felt it rumble through her own chest, causing her to smile even though she was clearly not in on the joke.

She couldn't help but notice that once again, Joe had appeared just when she needed him.

"So what brings you here?" Uncle Stan asked.

"Cupcakes. Well, that, and it's my turn to check up on Angie," Joe said. "Don't tell her I said that, though, or she'll get cranky. Hey, have you tried their Blonde Bombshell? It's amazing."

Mel felt herself flush with pleasure, but Uncle Stan exchanged an uncertain look with Rayburn and then nodded.

"Joe, can I have a word with you?" he asked. "Outside?"

"Sure," he said and turned to Mel. "Tell Ange to save me one of those raspberry things out there. You've got a crowd, and they're going fast."

"Will do." Mel tried not to feel abandoned when they disappeared, leaving her with the gangly detective.

Rayburn asked her about the flavors of the cupcakes she'd made for Christie, when she'd made them, and if she had a list of ingredients. He also asked if she had any more, and she went into the walk-in to check. There were a few of each. She showed the detective and then watched in horror as he pulled on gloves and bagged the cupcakes. This could not be good.

When Joe came back, he didn't look as if he'd been laughing. She felt nervous again, as if something was happening but no one was telling her exactly what.

"I think we're done here, Mel," Uncle Stan said. "If you think of anything I ought to know, call me."

"I will," she said as she gave him a quick hug.

"I'll walk this disgrace to the culinary arts out," Joe said, and then turned back. "Don't forget my cupcake."

"Oh, right." Mel went to the display case. She tried to see through the window, but they went the other way. Damn

"What's going on?" Angie asked, not bothering to hide her concern.

"I don't know," Mel answered. "They had a lot of questions about the cupcakes I made for Christie."

"That can't be good."

"No," Mel agreed. "Lucky thing Joe showed up."

"Lucky, my foot," Angie said. "As soon as Uncle Stan said it was business, I called Joe."

"You did?"

"Heck, yeah. What's the point of having an assistant district attorney brother if you can't call him in a crisis?"

"I don't know if this qualifies as a crisis, but I appreciate it."

"I hate to say it, but I'm getting a bad feeling about all of this, Mel," Angie said.

Mel looked at her and noticed that her large brown eyes looked flat-out scared. It made a shiver run up Mel's spine, but she shook it off. This was ridiculous. She hadn't done anything but bake some cupcakes and be the unfortunate one to find Christie. Surely everyone could see that?

When Joe returned, he looked as if he'd just witnessed a three-car pileup with no survivors.

"Mel," he said, "can I talk to you?"

"Sure." She followed him back to the kitchen.

"The medical examiner's preliminary findings are that Christie died of unnatural causes," he said.

"What?" Mel asked stupidly.

"She was a thirty-two-year-old female in excellent health with no preexisting conditions. Young women don't just drop dead. They'll be doing a full autopsy to discover the exact cause of death, but right now they suspect foul play was involved."

Mel sat down hard on one of the stools. She couldn't believe this. Christie had not been one of her favorite people by any stretch of the imagination, but murder? That seemed an awfully harsh way to go for being a self-involved egomaniac.

Joe sat on the stool beside her. She took comfort in his presence. He was the righter of wrongs. He'd always been like that. When any of his brothers got into a scuffle, Joe, born smack in the middle of the seven boys, was the one who stuck up for the underdog and negotiated a truce. It was small wonder that he had become a lawyer.

Mel couldn't help but wonder who he believed was the underdog here, however, her or Christie?

"What's going to happen?" she asked.

"In a nutshell, the detectives will investigate, the medical examiner will tell them what he discovers, they'll compile a suspect list, and when they gather enough evidence, they'll make an arrest. Then my office will prosecute the case, hopefully putting the murderer behind bars."

"Seems pretty clear-cut," Mel said.

"It should be, but it never is."

"Joe, am I going to need a lawyer?" she asked. Her voice sounded fainter than she would have liked, so she cleared her throat.

"Do *you* think you need a lawyer?" he countered.

Mel glanced at him and noticed his usually warm brown eyes were narrowed in concentration as he studied her. He could not possibly think that she did it!

She jumped to her feet. "I did not harm Christie!"

"I never said you did," he replied, jumping to his feet, too.

They faced each other with just a foot of space between them. Mel was so furious she was surprised she wasn't letting off sparks. First her mother then Uncle Stan, and now Joe—they all thought she was a suspect. It cut deep, and she was out of Band-Aids.

"Get out," she snapped. If he thought this badly of her, then she didn't want him around, no matter how much she liked him.

"Listen," he said. His voice was placating, but Mel was having none of it.

"No!" she snapped. She turned on her heel and stomped to her office. She slammed the door so hard it rattled on its hinges.

She heard Angie's voice through the door. It was muffled, but she could tell that Angie was irate. She heard Joe reply, but couldn't make out his words. It helped to know that her friend was on her side. She refused to acknowledge how much it hurt for Joe to think that she might be a murderer. It just showed that he didn't know her at all, not even one little bit.

She sat at her desk, and a picture of Angie, Tate, and herself stared back at her. It was from last Halloween when they had gone as the Three Stooges. She looked at Tate with his faux bald head—he'd been Curly—and she felt as if a giant hand was squeezing her chest. To lose his bride to a murderer, what must he be going through right now?

She dug her cell phone out of her purse. She needed to call him. His phone rang and rang and rang and went to voice mail.

"I've already tried three times."

Angie stood in the doorway.

"Did Joe tell you what the medical examiner thinks?"

"That Christie was murdered?" Angie asked. "Yes."

"Did he tell you they think I did it?"

"He didn't have to," Angie replied. "You found the body. It's not a big shock that they'd look at you."

"Whose side are you on?"

"Yours, duh," Angie said. "I'm just saying, of course they're going to look at you and, of course, they're wrong."

"Thank you, but it doesn't change the fact that someone did murder Christie."

"Do you think they're considering Tate?" Angie asked.

"He is . . . was her fiancé," Mel said. "I think they'd have to."

"It wasn't Tate," Angie said.

"I know"

"Then who?"

"How should I know?" Mel asked. "I barely knew the woman."

"No need to get snippy," Angie answered. "I was just throwing it out there."

"Yeah, well, a few too many people are looking at me for answers I don't have," Mel said. "It's making me cranky."

"So I see."

Mel gave her a look, but Angie just raised her eyebrows, the picture of innocence.

"You know who had a perverse reaction to Christie's death?" Mel asked.

Angie shook her head as she sank into the seat opposite the desk.

"The creepy-looking girl who came to pick up the cupcakes."

"Alma? I'd think death would be right up her alley. Probably it'll inspire her to greater heights of ghoulish fashion design."

"She wasn't surprised," Mel said, remembering the girl's callous reaction. "In fact, she almost seemed to have expected someone to murder Christie."

"You met with her for half an hour and you were ready to do her an injury," Angie pointed out. She reached up and tightened the band that held her thick hair in a ponytail on top of her had. "Can you imagine if you worked with her day in, day out?"

"So, you think it may have been someone in the design studio?"

"Maybe," Angie replied. "I suppose it depends on what kind of boss she was."

"I wonder if I could ask Alma," Mel said. "Or maybe Phoebe; she worshipped Christie."

"There's an accurate account," Angie's sarcasm was thicker than cream cheese frosting, but Mel ignored her.

"If I talk to both of them, I might get a better idea of what she was like to work for," Mel said.

The bells on the front door jangled, and Angie hopped up from her seat.

"The first thing you should do is talk to Tate," Angie said. "He'll have more information, plus you don't want to go digging up stuff on his fiancée that might hurt him."

Mel watched her go. She hated to think that this situation might put her friendship with Tate in jeopardy. Still, she couldn't have people thinking she was capable of murder. If everyone was looking at her, then they weren't looking at whoever really did it. And if they weren't going to, then someone had to, and since it was her neck in the noose, it looked like it was going to be her.

Eight

Unable to concentrate, Mel went to help Angie in the front of the shop. When she caught sight of their customers, however, she tried to scurry back to the office to hide. She would have made it, too, if Angie hadn't seen her and grabbed her arm, locking her into place.

"Hi, Mel," Dom DeLaura said. He was frowning. Next to him, wearing a matching grim expression to go with his mailman uniform was Ray DeLaura. They were Angie's two oldest brothers, and Mel was only surprised that the other five weren't in attendance as well.

"Hi, Dom, Ray," she said. A swift glance at Angie and she could tell the conversation was not going well.

"We came by to check on Angie," Dom said. "In light of recent events, we were thinking she might want to reconsider giving up her teaching position at Pueblo Elementary."

"One call to the district and you could have your job back," Ray said.

"I don't want my job back, I'm happy here."

"But we heard from a reliable source that there's been trouble, that one of your customers died," Dom said. "I can get you back on staff at the school immediately."

"Who died?" Angie spluttered. Apparently, she was giving a go at playing stupid. Mel wondered if it would work better for Angie with her brothers than it had with her own mother.

"You know, that bride, Christie what's-her-name," Ray said. "We heard she choked on a razor blade in one of your cupcakes."

Angie and Mel exchanged an outraged look. That was South Scottsdale for you. News traveled fast, especially if it was unsubstantiated, rumor-filled gossip.

"Did you hear this from Joe?" Mel asked. She felt betrayed, although why, she couldn't imagine. Joe DeLaura had a right to blab to whomever he wanted.

"No." Ray shook his head. "You know how he is. He wouldn't verify anything. No, this was from Xiuhau Lee. She delivered takeout to the detectives and heard them talking. She told me about it when I dropped off her mail."

"You don't want to be involved in this, Angie," Dom said. "You could have a nice career with the district."

Dom was on the school board, and he had pull. Mel knew that he and the other brothers liked Angie being a teacher. She was surrounded by kids and rarely met any men. It kept their lives free from worrying about her having any kind of a life.

"I had a wonderful career with the district, and now I have a new and equally wonderful career here," she said.

"But . . ." Ray interrupted.

"No buts," Angie snapped. "Listen, Christie did not die from one of our cupcakes, and there was no razor blade. She was my best friend's fiancée. I don't know what happened or how or why, but I do know that it doesn't matter if

I'm a teacher or a cupcake baker. Either way, I'm involved because I care about my friend. Now either order some cupcakes or make like a tree and leave!"

Dom's eyebrows shot up, and Ray looked like he was going to yell back. Luckily, the front door chimed and a group of high school kids walked in and filled the tables. The brothers were forced to take their arguments and their cupcakes to go.

Mel and Angie watched as they left in Ray's mail truck.

"I'm only surprised it took them this long." Angie sighed. In response to Mel's unasked question, she said, "And no, I have no interest in leaving the shop to go back to teaching."

Mel wisely let it go, for now.

She tried calling Tate three more times that day. He never answered, but at eight o'clock, just as she was flipping the Open sign to Closed, he appeared, looking haggard and spent.

She opened the door wide and he stumbled in. Angie took one look at his face and went to get him a cup of coffee.

Tate slid into a booth by the window and Mel closed the blinds, giving them privacy from any passersby. Angie returned with the coffee, and Tate nodded his thanks.

"How are you?" Mel asked as she and Angie slid into the booth seat across from him.

"It doesn't seem real," he said. "I keep thinking that it's a nightmare and I'm going to wake up, but then, I don't."

"Is there anything we can do?" Angie asked.

"I wish. Her parents are beside themselves. She was their only child."

"The police were here," Mel said.

Tate looked up at her. He looked confused. "Here? Why?"

"Uncle Stan didn't say as much, but they were gathering evidence." She was unable to keep the hurt out of her voice.

"Evidence of what?"

"Tate, they suspect foul play. They think Christie was murdered."

"What? But why? Who would want to harm her?"

Mel exchanged a look with Angie before she forged ahead. "Apparently, me."

"You?" Tate shook his head. "But that's ridiculous. You would never harm anyone, and certainly not the girl I am . . . was about to marry."

The verb tense seemed to throw him, and he turned his head to stare at the blinds while he gathered his composure.

Mel studied his profile and felt the warmth of his friendship, of his absolute faith in her, bubble up inside of her. He believed in her. It meant more to her than she could ever say.

"Tate, I hate to ask, but do you know anyone who might have been angry with Christie?"

He looked at her. His face was a picture of confusion. Then he sighed. It rumbled up from deep inside of him and blew across the table.

"Look, I know Christie was not the easiest person," he said. Mel felt Angie stiffen beside her. She hoped Angie had the good sense to keep her opinion to herself. "And I know you two might have had doubts about my marrying her, but I really appreciate the fact that you never said anything."

Angie reached across the table and put her hand over his. "We're your friends," she said. "Of course, we supported you—we always will."

Tate met Angie's gaze, and a tiny smile tipped one corner of his mouth.

"Thanks," he said.

As they gazed at each other, Mel had the weird sensation of being an outsider looking in. She'd never felt that way with the two of them before. It was always the three of them, bonded together, against the world.

She had the sinking feeling that it was because she was a suspect. Even though Tate had firmly and vocally denied any possibility that it could be her, she still felt tainted by suspicion, and she didn't like it one little bit.

Then Tate reached across the table and took her hand in his free one, and his kind eyes skimmed over her face.

"Thank you, too, Mel," he said. "I can't even imagine how awful this morning must have been for you. I'm so sorry."

"I only wish I'd gotten there sooner," she said. "Maybe I . . ."

Tate's cell phone rang, interrupting her. He let go of their hands while he fished it out of his pocket. He glanced at the screen and said, "It's my father. I have to go. I'll call you later."

They both nodded.

He rose from the booth, but then turned around and looked steadily at Mel. "Don't beat yourself up. There was nothing you could have done."

Mel nodded and watched him go.

Angie glanced at her. "What are you thinking?"

"That there was nothing I could do this morning, but that doesn't mean I can't help now."

"How?" Angie asked.

"I'm going to find out who had a grudge against Christie."

"Excellent," Angie said. "Where do we start?"

"Not we. Me."

Angie huffed, but Mel was firm. "You're not a suspect. I am. I don't want you dragged into this."

"But," Angie protested, sounding just like her brothers.
Mel cut her off. "No buts. You need to be there for
Tate."

Angie looked as if she'd argue, but then relented.

"So, who are you going to talk to first?"

"Oh, that's easy," Mel said. "The hostile one, Alma."

\'/\'/\'

After saying good night to Angie, Mel climbed the
back stairs to her apartment above the shop. It was a tiny
studio apartment, but it kept her from having to pay rent on
a residence as well as the shop. She had a tiny kitchenette,
a modest living room that doubled as her bedroom, and of
course, there was a petite bathroom as well.

She opened her refrigerator and took out the fixings for
a salad. As much as she loved her sweets and could eat
frosting by the bowlful, sometimes she just had to chomp
on some greens to keep her body from completely congeal-
ing into a large, sugary mass.

She diced an already broiled chicken breast and several jalapeno-stuffed olives. She dumped them on a bed
of romaine lettuce and grated some fresh Parmesan. She
drizzled oil and vinegar over the top and carried the bowl
to the café table in the corner of the apartment. She put the
bowl to one side and opened her laptop.

She had a wireless router in her office below, allowing
her access to the Internet up here. She took a bite of salad
while she waited for her laptop to connect.

It was fine to say that she was going to chat up Alma, but
there were some problems. First, she didn't know Alma's
last name. Second, she was pretty sure the studio would
be closed for a few days, so it wasn't as if she could track
Alma down there. Third, she had no idea what sort of reception she'd get from Alma if she did track her down.

Still, she was betting Christie would have a Web site, and she figured that, as a designer, Alma must be listed on the site somewhere.

Mel used Google to search "Christie Stevens Designs," making sure to put the words in quotation marks so the search engine would follow the exact word string. She couldn't hazard a guess as to how many Christies or Stevenses or even Christie Stevenses inhabited the Internet, but she knew that if she narrowed it to any Web page that specifically listed Christie Stevens Designs, then she'd get a match.

Sure enough, she got several hundred hits. A quick scan showed that many of the hits were for articles written about Christie's work, or for items of hers for auction on eBay, and so on. But the first hit did the trick, and Mel clicked the link to Christie's home page.

The Web page opened to a picture of her Scottsdale studio with a link to her Los Angeles studio. Mel scanned through Christie's bio and the virtual fashion show of her latest designs. She clicked on the About Us link, hoping that would profile the other designers, but no. There was nothing but Christie's glaring white smile from page to page to page.

Mel was sure that Phoebe and Alma had said they were designers. Why weren't they mentioned? Surely, they had to have been given credit for their work. Maybe they were just apprentices. Either way, Mel was out of luck since she hadn't gotten any listing on Alma or even verification of her existence on Christie's site.

She sat back in her chair and thoughtfully chewed on her salad. There had to be a way to track her. She went back to Google's main search page. She tried several variations of Alma and Christie Stevens until finally she found a blurb in a newspaper from Lubbock, Texas. It read that Alma Rodriguez had taken a job with Christie

Stevens Designs. There was a picture of a lovely girl with a bright smile and laughing eyes. The caption was Alma's name, but Mel had a hard time reconciling the smiling girl in the photo with the black-clad, dour woman she had met. Is that what working for Christie had done to the poor girl?

Now that she had Alma's name, she grabbed the phone book by her bed and looked her up. There were four pages of Rodriguezes listed. Six had the first name Alma. Mel ruled out the ones that had addresses on the west side of town. That would be too far a commute. She pulled out a map and marked the three that were located closest to Christie's studio. She called the first one. A recorded male voice told her to leave a message. She called the second one.

On the third ring a terse voice answered, "Yeah?"

"Alma? It's Melanie Cooper, from the cupcake bakery," she said.

There was a beat of silence and then, "What do you want?"

Mel took this to mean she had the right Alma. The surlitude certainly matched the Alma she knew.

"I want to talk to you about Christie," she said.

"What for?"

"The police believe that her death wasn't an accident," Mel said.

"Yeah, I know. Shocker."

Mel took a deep breath in through her nose. Alma's hostility was beginning to grate on her nerves.

"I'd like to talk to you about it."

"Why?"

"Because I have some questions."

"Don't we all?"

"Look," Mel said, her patience at an end. "She was engaged to my best friend. He's really messed up about her death, and I'm trying to help him. Now, do you think you could meet me for a cup of coffee or not?"

"Tate Harper is your friend?"

"Yes."

Alma was silent and then growled, "When and where?"

"How about Java Jive at nine o'clock tomorrow?"

"Fine," Alma agreed, and hung up. She sounded as enthusiastic as a person committing to a colonoscopy.

Mel stared at the phone in her hand. She wondered if she should call Phoebe, too. Then again, Phoebe seemed to be taking Christie's death much harder than Alma. Perhaps she should give her some time and find out what Alma had to say first.

She hung up the phone. She would have liked to call Tate, but she didn't want to disturb him. She couldn't imagine what he was feeling.

Her thoughts skimmed over the day. She flashed on finding Christie's body, dealing with her mother and Uncle Stan, and the empathy she felt for Tate. Then she thought about Joe and how angry she'd been at him.

She swabbed the bottom of her salad bowl with the last chunk of chicken, cleaning up the cheese and dressing before popping it into her mouth.

She knew her anger with Joe had been disproportionate to the conversation they'd been having. It really wasn't his fault that he viewed today's events from the mind-set of a prosecutor. Angie always said he was known as a junkyard dog in the courtroom, which was why he was so successful. Mel just hadn't expected him to turn that part of his persona toward her.

She didn't need to be told that it looked bad for her to be the one who found the body. And she knew that it was her own guilt, the fact that she had really disliked Christie, that made her feel oversensitive to being fingered as a suspect.

As if she could be guilty just because she really didn't want her friend to marry such an egomaniacal harpy. Sheesh, now she felt guilty for thinking badly about Christie.

She wondered if she should call Joe to apologize. She rejected the idea immediately. First of all, what would she say? And second of all, he still made her nervous, and she really wasn't up for making a stuttering, stammering ass of herself.

She'd wait until they bumped into each other someday, and hopefully, the awkwardness would have passed. It could be months or even years until she saw him again. Unless, of course, she was arrested for murder; then she'd be seeing him again all too soon. The thought did not comfort.

She shut off her laptop and took her salad bowl to the sink.

If she was meeting Alma at nine, she'd better get some shut-eye. She rinsed her bowl and glanced out at the street below. Old Town was just settling in for the night. It was almost ten o'clock. The restaurants were serving their last customers and art galleries had already closed. A few bars were scattered amidst the quaint shops, and they would stay open until two in the morning.

It had taken Mel a few months to adjust to the noise that came with living in the middle of one of the most popular nightspots in the Valley of the Sun, but now she wondered if she'd be able to sleep without it.

She pushed aside the lace-trimmed curtain that covered the window above her kitchen sink. The streetlights illuminated the cobbled walkway below, and she saw an elderly couple walking hand in hand towards the public parking lot around the corner. A group of young men—she guessed by their AF attire that they were college students—were headed in the other direction.

She was about to let the curtain fall when she saw another person, standing half in the shadow of the overhang across the street. She couldn't tell if it was a man or a woman, but judging by the way her hair prickled on the back of her neck, she knew the person was watching her.

She wanted to jump back from the window, but a latent cautious streak made her pause, as if everything were perfectly normal. Her heart was knocking around in her chest like a newly caged animal desperate for escape. She inhaled through her nose and slowly exhaled from between pursed lips. She let the curtain fall with her exhale as if it were part of a yoga posture.

Who was out there in the dark watching her?

What could they want with her? Was it a cop? No, a cop would come to the door. Was it a burglar? Ridiculous. Who would rob a cupcake bakery when there were so many art galleries and jewelry stores in the area?

She could feel her fingers tremble. This was ridiculous. It was probably just a smoker who had wandered away from one of the restaurants to maintain the state-mandated twenty-foot distance between himself and the door.

She was just overwrought from finding Christie's body today, and obviously it was making her paranoid and twitchy. She thought about peeking through the curtain again but rejected the idea. Of course, there was no reason she couldn't take her trash out and see who might be loitering on the street. Just to reassure herself, of course.

Mel grabbed the half-full bag of trash from under the kitchen sink. She opened the fridge and stuffed in some expired boxes of takeout just to make the bag seem fuller. She took her house key from the hook on the wall and let herself out the back door.

A quick glance at the alley below told her it was empty. She would simply throw her bag in the Dumpster and then stroll around the building to see who might be lurking. It had to be done; otherwise she'd never sleep tonight.

She hurried down the stairs, slipping her key into her pocket as she went. She tossed the bag into the Dumpster. It made a crunch as it hit the other bags already inside, and the stench of sour milk hit her nose like a punch. She eased the metal lid down to keep it from banging.

She wiped her hands on the back of her jeans and took a deep breath. Fairy Tale Cupcakes was housed in its own building, and she had a very narrow walkway on either side of it that gave her access to the front of the building. She went down the left side of the building because there was more light on that side.

Halfway down the walkway, the street became visible. She stared at the spot where she had seen the person skulking in the shadows. It was too dark to tell if anyone was there now. She slowed her pace to give herself more time to study the spot.

"Hey!" a man yelled, and Mel jumped, bumping into the wall at her right.

A woman, clutching a cowboy hat in her hand, sprinted by the alley with a laugh as the man chased after her with a grin.

Mel was thrilled to see they were having a good time. Really.

She shook her head and strode forward. Enough. She wasn't going to be some timid little mouse. She stepped onto the well-lit sidewalk and started to cross the street.

A hand grabbed her elbow just as a trolley bus rolled by. Mel whipped around to slug whoever had grabbed her, and discovered it was Joe DeLaura.

"Are you nuts?" he yelled. "You almost walked right in front of that bus."

That reminded Mel of her purpose, and she yanked her arm out of his hold and darted across the street.

"Mel, where are you going?" he called after her, but she ignored him.

No one stood under the awning. Damn it! She had been so sure.

She jogged up and down the sidewalk but there was no one. At the corner, a small courtyard was closed off by an iron gate. Mel noticed the gate was still swinging, as if someone had run through it. She glanced into the court-yard shared by three little shops. They were closed for the night and the cobblestoned space was empty.

"Do you have a death wish?" Joe yelled when he caught up to her.

She glared at him.

"Sorry, probably not a good day to pose a question like that, huh?"

"You think?"

"What are you looking for?" he asked.

"I thought I saw someone watching me."

"What?" Joe's gaze met hers. "Where? When?"

"You forgot who," she said. She turned away from the courtyard feeling bitterly disappointed. She didn't know why, but she felt that catching the person watching her shop was important, very important.

"No, I didn't," he said. "I assumed if you knew who, you would have said as much."

"Oh." She'd have to give him that one, but she wasn't happy about it. She crossed the street and checked the front of the bakery. The door was shut and locked, and none of the windows were smashed. She circled the building.

Joe shadowed her. She was torn between being irritated with him and grateful for the backup. She knew he wasn't going to go away until his questions were answered. Well, he'd just have to wait. First, she wanted to check her build-ing. She didn't know what she was checking for, but she knew she'd sleep better if she had a clear picture of the building in her mind.

Once she finished checking all of the nooks and crannies, Mel stopped at the bottom of the stairs to her studio apartment and turned to face Joe.

"So, what are you doing here at this time of night?"

"Would you believe I had a hankering for a cupcake?" he asked.

Nine

"No," Mel said. She wanted her voice to sound stern and huffy, but instead it came out giggly and amused. How very annoying.

In her own defense, it was hard to stay mad at a man who looked at her from beneath a thick fringe of lashes and whose crooked smile let her know he was feeling chagrined.

"Well, it was worth a try," he said. "Actually, I was in the area having dinner with a colleague, and I thought I'd stop by and apologize. I realized, when I got back to my office, that I sounded accusatory towards you, and I didn't mean to be. It's just the nature of my work to always be looking for the guilty party."

"Angie ripped you to shreddle, didn't she?"

"I'm going to have scars," he confirmed.

"Serves you right," Mel said with a laugh. "But thank you for the apology."

Silence fell between them. The soft glow of a distant

streetlight illuminated the back of Joe's head and Mel had a hard time making out his features, but she knew he was looking at her, studying her.

"Mel, if you think of anything about today, about finding Christie, that you think is relevant, I want you to call me."

"Okay," she said. She took the card that he fished out of his pocket.

"This is going to be a very high-profile case," he said. "Beware of the press and anyone else who asks you questions."

"I assume that 'anyone' means anyone but you," she said.

His grin flashed white in the night. "You assume correct."

There was nothing left to say, yet Mel was reluctant to climb the stairs to her apartment.

"Joe?" a woman's voice called from the alley. It was followed by the unmistakable sound of high heels clacking against the cement walkway towards them.

The woman stepped into the light, and Mel wasn't sure what struck her first: her twig-thin figure in a curve-hugging skirt and blue silk blouse, the copper highlights in her long, wavy mahogany hair, or her full lips painted a lovely plum color and set perfectly in her heart-shaped face.

She looped her hand around Joe's elbow as if she needed him for balance, but Mel suspected it was really more a possession is nine-tenths of the law sort of thing. Mel knew that move. She'd used it herself.

"Susan," Joe said with a smile, "meet Melanie Cooper. She owns Fairy Tale Cupcakes with my little sister, Angie."

"Oh." Susan's brown eyes went wide, and she loosened her hold on Joe. "It's nice to meet you."

Mel shook her outstretched hand. She couldn't help but

notice that Susan had a perfect manicure, French tips on hands that were as soft as butter. She felt like shoving her own short-nailed, dry-skinned paws into her pockets, but she didn't.

"Mel, this is Susan Ross. She's a colleague of mine," Joe said.

The lovely brunette tossed her hair over her shoulder and gazed up at Joe. She gushed, "Oh, we're more than that, aren't we, Joe?"

Joe smiled down at her, and the brunette snuggled back up against him. Mel wished she had a bowl of buttercream frosting and a spatula handy. It had done wonders on Olivia's van; she could only imagine what it would do to these two.

There wasn't anything more to be said, so she wished them both a good night and skedaddled up to her apartment. She could hear Susan's laughter echoing in the alley behind her.

~·~·~

Mel was awake before her mother keyed into her apartment. Not only was she awake, she was slurping coffee and reading the newspaper.

Her mother blinked at her and glanced around the small apartment, as if looking for something that needed doing to justify her presence.

"Coffee, Mom?" Mel asked.

"Why, yes, thank you," Joyce said. "That would be lovely."

Mel rose from her seat and retrieved a white ceramic mug from the cupboard above the coffeepot while her mother sat at the small table in the corner.

"You're up awfully early," Joyce said. "Did you have trouble sleeping?"

"I slept like a baby." She did not mention it was more like a colicky baby with sleep issues.

The few dreams she'd had centered on the image of Christie's leg sticking out from under her designer gowns, followed by visions of Joe DeLaura glaring at her from the prosecutor's table while she sat on the witness stand on a seat that resembled a bed of nails. Before she could stop it, a shudder ran through her.

Mel glanced over her shoulder and saw her mother reading the headlines of the *Arizona Republic*.

"They didn't get your good side," Joyce said as she pushed the paper away.

"I don't have a good side," Mel retorted.

She had retrieved her paper this morning and found that a large color photo of herself hugging Tate at the crime scene was the focal point of the lead story, which of course was Christie's murder. Without saying as much, the paper managed to make her longtime friendship with Tate sound seedy and suspect.

Her temper had boiled at the reporter's innuendo-laden story. She had scrutinized the article line by line, and realized that the reporter had written a tabloid-worthy story that she couldn't refute, because it was all speculation and no hard facts.

Damn it! She could only imagine how this was going to make Tate feel. The thought of him suffering for their friendship made Mel's temper flare again, and she had to force herself to breathe in slowly and try to calm down.

"I made an appointment with Johnny Dietz for you," Joyce said.

Mel put her mother's coffee in front of her and resumed her own seat at the table.

"Any particular reason?" she asked, fighting to keep her voice even.

"You need a lawyer," her mother said.

"No, I don't, I didn't do anything wrong."

"They're going to come after you," Joyce said, her voice trembling. "You need to protect yourself."

"Mom, Johnny Dietz is a tax attorney."

"Your father used him for years," Joyce said. "Our taxes were always perfect, never any audits, not one."

Mel had to look down at the table to keep from laughing. She supposed it was probably hysterics, but still, the thought of Johnny Dietz, in all his round and bald glory, going nose to nose with Joe DeLaura gave her a severe case of the giggles.

"Something is funny?" Joyce asked. "A young woman is dead, and you're the prime suspect. I don't see what's so funny."

Duly rebuked, Mel felt her smile slink off the side of her face like a misbehaving puppy putting its tail between its legs.

"Sorry, Mom," she said. "I appreciate that you're looking out for me, I do."

Joyce sniffed and opened another section of the paper. "Your horoscope is only giving you a one-star day. I'd go back to bed if I were you."

After her mother left, Mel called Angie and told her about her appointment with Alma. Angie offered to come along, but Mel figured she'd best keep this meeting one on one, so Alma didn't feel ganged up on. She really didn't know what information she was going to get out of the surly designer, but she had to try for Tate's sake, if not her own.

She hurried through her shower. Alma was a fashion designer, so she knew there was no way she was going to intimidate the young woman with her extensive wardrobe

of jeans and T-shirts, but she still needed her outfit to set
the tone. She thought back to her days as a marketing exec.
When trying to woo a client, the firm researched the company thoroughly. If its execs dressed in Armani, so did Mel
and her team. It was a basic rapport builder.

She doubted she had time to dye her short blonde hair
black, but she could definitely throw together an ensemble
worthy of Elvira, Queen of the Night, though perhaps with
less cleavage showing, lots less.

Mel donned her black Hilfiger jeans and a black, long-
sleeved T-shirt that she'd picked up at Target. Black Con-
verse All Stars and a heavy hand with her black eyeliner,
and she was ready. A glance in the mirror told her she
looked somewhat scary. She hoped it was in a good way.

Java Jive was around the corner on Marshall Way,
wedged between a falafel house and an art gallery. The
interior of the place was dark, as if trying to maintain the
illusion of night and not offend those of its clientele who
were not yet ready to face the day. Mel crossed the scarred
wooden floor as the distinct aroma of burnt coffee grounds
saturated her senses. The only lighting in the place was
from blue neon tracks that ran along the ceiling, giving the
room just enough light to keep patrons from bumping into
the furniture.

Mel scoped the place, hoping to be sitting before Alma
arrived. A glance at a small square table in the corner, however, told her that her date had arrived before her, probably
with the same intention. No matter.

Mel rolled her shoulders and wove her way through
the sea of small café tables to the corner. Alma didn't
bother to glance up, although Mel was sure she'd seen her
approaching.

"Hi, Alma," she said. "Thanks for meeting me."

Alma put aside the issue of *Vogue* and swept Mel from
head to foot with her gaze. As if aware of her strategy,

Alma lifted the corner of her mouth in a small sneer and said, "Nice."

Mel took the seat opposite her. The table wobbled when she plunked her purse on it, so she moved her bag onto the seat next to her.

A waitress with cranberry-colored spiked hair and a nose ring paused at their table.

"Hi, welcome to Java Jive. What can I get you?" she asked.

"A latte, please," Mel said.

Alma had an espresso already in front of her, and shook her head to let the waitress know she was fine.

"What do you want to know?" Alma asked. She glanced at her watch.

"You have someplace to be?" Mel asked.

Alma stared at her. Her dark brown eyes were rimmed with kohl, and her foundation was several shades lighter than her skin tone. Her inky black hair was styled in careless spikes, and she wore a black knit bodysuit with a black leather minidress over it. If they were in a morgue, Mel would have thought someone had left a body bag unzipped.

"I have a job interview," Alma said.

"What about the studio?" Mel asked.

"It's closed," Alma said. "I have no idea who Christie's beneficiary is, and I'm not sticking around to find out. As far as I'm concerned, my contract with Christie is now null and void. I'm free."

"Free?" Mel repeated. "Interesting choice of words."

They were silent as the waitress returned with Mel's latte. She stirred in a packet of sugar and glanced up at Alma, who was considering her through a narrowed gaze.

"Don't read anything into it," Alma said. "I didn't murder Christie. It's just that my contract with her was more binding than I realized upon signing."

"When would it have expired?" Mel asked.

"I was locked into a five-year contract," Alma said. "I had three to go."

"Wasn't working for Christie Stevens a coup?" Mel asked. "I mean, she's international, Paris runways and all of that."

"She's an up-and-comer, or at least she was," Alma agreed.

"But?" Mel encouraged her to continue.

"But the only one getting any attention at her studio was Christie. Phoebe and I created the looks and Christie put her name on them."

"Surely, she . . ."

"No," Alma interrupted. Her brown eyes were narrowed with anger. "Christie was the head of the company, but she didn't design anything. She collected the CFDA awards and the accolades, but the vision and the talent belonged to me and Phoebe."

"Sounds like you hated her," Mel said.

"Pretty much. In the beginning it was an honor to work for her, but when I saw my sketches, my ideas, become hers, I realized she was stealing my work and calling it her own."

"How did Phoebe feel about it?" Mel asked. "Was she as angry as you?"

Alma shook her head, her lip curled in disgust. "She worshipped Christie. She'd have given up her firstborn if Christie asked for it. It was sickening."

"You realize you have a pretty strong motive to want Christie dead," Mel said.

"That's what the cops said," Alma agreed. "But I have an alibi for the entire night, and they seem to be focusing on another angle, a love triangle sort of thing."

A nasty smile played around her lips, and Mel felt all of the blood drain from her face. She hadn't had the warm fuzzies for Alma before, but now she felt it was safe to say that she actively disliked the young woman.

"Yeah, well, when they discover they're wrong, I imagine they'll come back to you," Mel said. She made her voice saccharine sweet when she added, "I think they'll find it quite interesting that you were the one who delivered the cupcakes from my shop to Christie, and she was holding one when she died."

It was Alma's turn to become pale, which was an achievement, given the amount of pasty foundation she was wearing. Mel couldn't help but feel a flush of satisfaction at her discomfiture.

Alma scowled. "What's your point?"

"Work with me. If neither of us killed her, then who did?"

"How would I know?" Alma asked. "Christie had a lot of enemies. It could be anyone."

"Did she fight with anyone recently?"

"Daily," Alma replied.

Mel sighed. She was losing her patience. "Was there anyone who seemed angrier with her than usual?"

Alma stared into her half-empty cup. "Let's see. The models hated her, and so did the photographers. No one was ever pretty enough for her clothes, and she had constant battles with the photographers over their vision versus hers. Her rival Terry Longmore wasn't signing up for her fan club anytime soon. And for that matter, the wedding vendors were getting pretty snarky with all of her demands, too. The caterer told her he hoped she choked on a canapé right before he quit."

"Why?" Mel asked.

"Contract issues," Alma said. "Christie likes . . . liked to own everything. She wanted music written just for her and flower arrangements just for her. She wanted all of her vendors to sign contracts giving her ownership of their creations."

"So it wasn't just me," Mel said.

"Hardly. Christie had an obsessive need to own everything. It was almost pathologic, like she was afraid some crumb of fame might pass her by if she didn't get full credit for every single aspect of her life."

"Whoa," Mel said.

"She was a total head case." Alma watched Mel for a minute. "I've met your friend, Tate. He was always nice. What, exactly, did he see in her?"

"I wish I knew."

Alma nodded as if she understood, but how could she, when Mel didn't understand it herself?

Alma glanced at her watch and rose abruptly from her chair. "I have to go."

"Who's your interview with?"

"None of your business," Alma said. "It's been real."

Mel watched her walk away, and was surprised when Alma turned around and approached the table.

"Listen, the thing with Christie was going to happen one way or another," Alma said. "She was racking up enemies like some women collect shoes. The outcome was inevitable."

Then Alma turned and strode out of the coffee shop without a backward glance. Mel got the distinct impression that the young woman thought she had done "the thing with Christie" and was absolving her of the crime. She wanted to protest her innocence, but there was no one to hear her. Alma was gone, and none of the other customers were paying her any attention.

She paid for her half-finished latte and hurried back to Fairy Tale Cupcakes, needing to be comforted by the familiar for as long as she was able.

Ten

"She thinks I'm guilty," Mel said to Angie as they worked side by side in the kitchen, frosting their freshly baked and cooled Red Velvet cupcakes with thick smears of cream cheese icing.

Mel wanted to sit down and stuff four of them into her mouth in rapid succession, but the profit side of her business made her resist such temptation. Anything eaten was one less bought, so chowing down on the cupcakes was not only bad for her butt spread, but it didn't help business either.

"You have to wonder what the police think of her sparkling personality," Angie said. "I mean, she doesn't exactly hide how she felt about Christie. Don't you think that would make her suspect number one, whether she has an alibi or not?"

"I don't know," Mel replied. "All I can figure, is she must have a really good one."

"Did she give you any idea of anyone else who might have a motive?"

"The list was endless. Christie seemed to alienate everyone equally."

"To the point of murder?" Angie asked skeptically.

"I know," Mel said. "It doesn't make sense."

"What doesn't make sense?"

Both women turned towards the door to the shop. Framed in the doorway were Uncle Stan and his partner, Detective Rayburn.

Mel dropped her spatula into the bowl of frosting and wiped her hands on her apron. She crossed the room to give her uncle a quick hug. She wondered if it was just her imagination, or was he squeezing her a little tighter than usual?

"What can I do for you, Uncle Stan?"

"Actually, we're here to talk to Angie," he said.

Angie's eyes went round, and she glanced at Mel as if to ask, "What the . . . ?"

"Miss DeLaura?" Detective Rayburn prompted her.

Although it was ridiculous, Mel felt her ears grow hot, and her heart thumped loudly in her chest. She really did not like the cloud of suspicion that seemed to hover over her. She decided to bluff.

"Use the office," she suggested. "It'll be more private."

Uncle Stan gave her an approving nod, and Mel returned it with a weak smile.

They were going to find the small office a tight squeeze, but maybe that would move them on their way.

The door closed behind them and Mel could hear the low rumble of voices, but not any specific words, much to her chagrin. She slathered frosting on cupcakes, not really paying attention, while keeping her ears pricked up for words like "arrest" and "suspect," but still, she heard nothing.

She wondered if Joe knew that his sister was being questioned. She could only imagine how that was going to go over. If the brothers had been unhappy with Angie giving up teaching to hawk cupcakes before, this was going to send them into multiple tailspins of brotherly distress.

Unbidden, an image of the woman Joe had been with last night flashed into her mind. Susan Ross was obviously from his world, a girl lawyer who dressed in Elie Tahari and probably drove an Infiniti, who didn't know a spatula from a whisk and got all of her sustenance from takeout containers or leisurely dinners with her male coworkers.

Mel felt like an idiot for believing he'd been having dinner with his colleague and just thought he'd stop by. The man had been on a date. A date! She couldn't remember the last time she'd had a date.

She grabbed a spoon and scraped up the last of the rich, tangy frosting. She licked it off the spoon as if it were a big lollipop. She knew it was wrong to be eating for comfort, but there was no denying that at the moment, it made her feel better.

She had to accept the reality that Joe DeLaura was a handsome, successful attorney who undoubtedly had to beat the women off with his briefcase. This was not news. He'd always had a girlfriend in high school. In fact, she and Angie had made his life a misery by demanding to go to the movies with him and his dates. Mama DeLaura had loved the idea. Mel was pretty sure Joe had never gotten past first base on any of his dates, because she and Angie were always there to keep him in check. Small wonder he never let them come visit him in college.

The bells hanging on the front door of the shop jangled, and Mel went to greet her customers. Three four-packs of cupcakes later, she was back in the kitchen. She was just putting the Red Velvets on a tray when the office door opened.

"If you think of anything, call me," Uncle Stan said. Mel knew that tone. It wasn't a request.

Angie nodded, looking grim.

Mel put four cupcakes in a box and handed it to Uncle Stan. He looked as if he'd refuse, but she stepped away, giving him no choice but to take it with him.

"Thanks, Mel," he said. The outside door shut behind them.

With Angie's help Mel hefted the fresh tray of cupcakes out to the main room to restock the display case.

"Where were you after we finished watching the movie at Tate's?" Angie asked.

"I went home and went to bed," Mel said. "I was dead on my feet from being up all night the night before, coming up with new flavors for Christie. You know that."

"Yeah, I know that and you know that, but Uncle Stan's partner isn't buying it," she said. She sent a sour look in the direction of the door. "He wondered if I could provide an alibi for you or Tate. Mel, I'm afraid he thinks the two of you did this together."

"For what possible reason?" Mel asked. "If Tate didn't want to marry her, all he had to do was call it off."

"He didn't say as much, but I get the feeling there's a lot of pressure coming from Christie's father," Angie said. "Mr. Stevens wants an arrest, like yesterday."

"Melanie? Angela?" Only one person called Angie, Angela: Mel's mother.

Sure enough, with a click-clack of high heels, Joyce Cooper strode through the front door into the bakery. She was wearing a narrow, knee-length black skirt with a lime colored silk blouse underneath a matching black jacket. Her champagne-colored bob was swept back from her face, and at her ears and around her left wrist she wore black pearls. She looked like she was ready to start kicking butt and taking names.

"Angela, you look as lovely as always." Joyce hugged

Angie, she had always adored her, and then turned to hug Mel but frowned instead.

"Why aren't you dressed?" she asked.

Mel glanced down. Beneath her pink Fairy Tale Cupcakes apron, she still wore her black long-sleeved tee and black jeans. A little goth, perhaps, but it wasn't like she was in her pajamas.

"I am dressed," she said.

"Honestly!" Joyce rolled her eyes at Angie. "How do you put up with her?"

"Some days it's tough," Angie commiserated with a sigh. Mel stuck her tongue out at her.

"I saw that," Joyce said, although she still had her back to Mel.

Mel huffed out an exasperated breath. Some people claimed their mothers had eyes in the backs of their heads, but Joyce really did.

"Hurry," Joyce said as she spun back to her. "Our meeting is in twenty minutes, and you need to dress appropriately."

"What meeting?" Mel asked.

"With your attorney," Joyce said.

"You didn't."

"I told you I was going to."

Angie's head swiveled between them as if she were watching a tennis match.

"Johnny Dietz, the tax attorney?" Mel asked.

"Yes, and I don't want to hear it. He's a very competent attorney and he's willing to help for free," Joyce said.

Free? Mel hung her head. Joyce had game.

"Do you mind manning the shop alone for a little bit?" she asked Angie.

"Not at all," Angie said. She kept her head down, and Mel suspected it was because she was trying not to laugh.

"Wear a dress," her mother ordered. "It wouldn't hurt you to look like a lady every now and then."

Mel strode to the back door with her teeth clamped together. Before she left, she heard her mother ask, "Now, Angela, why is it I never hear about who you're dating? Surely a lovely young lady like yourself has loads of boyfriends."

Mel's teeth unclenched, and she grinned. It was refreshing to have Joyce home in on someone else for a change. Maybe she could convince her to adopt Angie. Either that, or she could get her a puppy. In any event, something had to give. She could not be her mother's only hobby.

Johnny Dietz's office sat in the basement of a commercial property on the edge of Old Town. Small businesses, with names that gave Mel no clue as to what they actually did, filled the squat, five-story building of tinted glass and stone.

She followed her mother down the stairs to Dietz's office. The receptionist offered them coffee or water, which they both declined, while they sat on the puffy brown couch and perused a collection of financial magazines that Mel thought would be grand for a night when she had a raging case of insomnia and CSPAN didn't do the trick.

In no time at all, Johnny Dietz shot out of a door behind the reception area and approached them with his hands outstretched, looking like an evangelist offering a conversion.

Joyce stood and let him take her hands in his. He kissed her cheek and Mel thought, Ew.

Dietz was short, fat, and bald. His pudgy right hand sported a diamond-encrusted pinky ring, and Mel noticed that he kept the finger extended as if to let the diamonds catch the light at every opportunity.

"Joyce, how good to see you," he said. "I was just delighted when I got your call. It's been too long."

"Yes, it has."

Mel noticed that her mother surreptitiously slid her hands out of his as soon as was socially acceptable to do so.

"And Melanie." Dietz turned to her and held out his hand. "Why, I haven't seen you since you were in pigtails."

Actually, she'd seen him at her father's funeral ten years ago, and she was fairly certain that at twenty-four, she hadn't been in pigtails, but she decided to let it go.

"Well, come in, come in," he said. "Let's go sit in my office and you can tell me what I can assist you with."

Mel looked goggle-eyed at her mother. "You didn't tell him?" she hissed.

"I didn't want to get into it over the phone," Joyce hissed back.

"Oh, my God," Mel said. "I'm in a nightmare, aren't I? Feel free to wake me up now."

"Now, now." Dietz smiled over his shoulder at her. "I'm sure it just seems like that. We'll get whatever it is all straightened out, don't you worry."

"Really?" Mel asked. "Because the homicide detectives, one of whom is my own uncle, seem to think the best way to straighten it out is to arrest me for murder."

"Um . . . I'm sorry. Homicide?" Dietz faltered as he pushed open the door to his office.

"How's your criminal law?" Mel asked as she walked past him.

"You're not a criminal," Joyce said as she followed her and sat in one of the two chairs opposite the large walnut desk.

A small sand garden with a delicate wooden rake rested on the front edge of the desk. Mel had a feeling that by the time they left, Dietz was gong to need a miniature John Deere to ease his stress.

He sat in his desk chair with an ominous creak and

swiveled to face them. His face was round and flushed. He glanced between the two of them and gave them a smile that was meant to be reassuring, but it was hard to pull off, given that he looked as alarmed as a man in over his head should.

"Perhaps you could get me up to speed," he said.

"The love of Mel's life was about to marry another," Joyce said. She bit her lip and looked at Mel with a pity usually reserved for the terminally ill. "And they hired Mel to make the cupcakes for their wedding, she made some samples, the bride ate one, and died. Now the police are investigating."

Dietz turned his head sideways to study Mel as if she were an abstract painting and he wasn't sure which side was up.

"It sounds worse than it is," Joyce tried to reassure him.

"And there are a couple of inaccuracies," Mel said. "First, he is not now, nor has he ever been, the love of my life."

Joyce opened her mouth to protest, but Mel held up her hand to nix the argument.

"Second, I don't think my cupcake had anything to do with her dying. She just happened to be holding it when I found her body."

Dietz blinked. He rose from his seat and flipped through his Rolodex. He quickly copied down a name and number on a blue Post-it.

"This is the best defense attorney in town," he said, handing the note to Joyce. "Call him."

"But . . ." Joyce began, but Dietz stayed in motion as he opened his office door and gestured them out.

"Great seeing you, really, don't be a stranger."

Mel and Joyce glanced at each other and slowly rose from their seats. There was no question they were dismissed.

As they crossed the parking lot, Joyce tucked the note into her purse. Once in the car, she turned the key and said, "Well, that was abrupt."

"Too bad," Mel said. "I think he wanted to ask you out, but you come with too much baggage."

Joyce looked at her. "Well, if he can't handle a murderess for a stepdaughter, what good is he?"

"Indeed."

They drove silently back to Fairy Tale Cupcakes. Joyce pulled into a spot down the sidewalk from the shop and turned to Mel.

"I'm worried about you," she said.

"Don't be. The police will find whoever did this. I'm sure of it."

Joyce looked as if she wanted to discuss it more. Instead, she said, "I'm calling the number Johnny gave us— just in case."

"That's because you're a good mom," Mel said. She leaned over and kissed her mother's cheek. "I'll call you later."

She waved as her mother drove away and then trotted back into the shop. Her happy hour cupcake class was meeting in a half hour, and she hadn't prepped tonight's project, the Mojito cupcake. It was another of her personal favorites, although weren't they all? The Mojito was a golden cupcake flavored with lime zest and dried spearmint leaves and topped with a rum-flavored icing.

Right about now Mel figured she could use a shot of rum icing—okay, maybe just the rum.

She hurried into the shop. Angie was waiting on three booths of customers and filling two takeout orders. Mel quickly donned her apron over her dress and began boxing up the next order.

"I baked the cupcakes for class tonight," Angie said as they darted past each other. "You just need to frost them."

"I love you," Mel said.

"Yeah? Then give me a raise," Angie teased.

"I'll double your salary."

"Wow. Really? Two times zero is what again?"

Mel grinned as she rang up the next customer. He was a tall gentleman with gray hair and kind blue eyes. She'd noticed he came in every Wednesday about this time. She glanced at the name on his bank card as she handed it back to him.

"Same time next week, Mr. Larson?" she asked.

"Absolutely," he said. "It's not bridge club if we don't have our Fairy Tale cupcakes."

Mel was hit again by the power of what she and Angie provided to their customers. Memories. When people bit into one of their cupcakes, they were enjoying a moment that recaptured the magic of childhood, nurtured their sweet tooth, and gave them something to share with a loved one.

Were they curing cancer? No. But were they making the world a better place to live in? Quite possibly. At least, Mel liked to think so. She couldn't imagine a world without cupcakes, and she hoped her customers couldn't either.

"Go frost," Angie said. "I've got it covered now."

"You sure?" Mel asked.

Angie nodded.

"I really do owe you a raise," Mel said.

"You can treat me to a spa day next quarter."

"You're on," Mel agreed.

She dashed up to her apartment to change into jeans and a Henley. She put her apron back on over that and hurried back down to the kitchen to frost the Mojito cupcakes.

She would have liked to use real dark rum in the buttercream frosting, but instead she used two tablespoons of rum extract. Once the frosting achieved its desired fluffy consistency, she put a dollop on each cupcake and then pressed in a candied spearmint leaf. With the silver cupcake liners

Angie had chosen, the effect was very partylike, and she knew her students would enjoy making these.

She was just wiping down the table when the first of her students arrived. Emily Dubrowski, newly from Chicago, and her cousin Claire Dubrowski were the first to enter the kitchen.

"Oh, my God." Emily unzipped her hooded jacket and draped it on a chair. "I love those."

She had a broad face, dusted with freckles, and a tiny turned-up nose. She was stout but not heavy, and wore a pair of thick glasses that she usually pushed up into her gray hair when she was concentrating on a recipe. Her cousin Claire looked exactly like her, but without the glasses. Their love of cooking and the art of cupcake baking made them two of Mel's favorites, although she tried not to show preferential treatment.

"Thanks, Emily," she said. Three more students wandered in and gushed over the cupcakes, and Mel put them to work at the Hobart mixer, as they would have to bake the cupcakes in a big batch in her industrial-sized convection oven in order to get everyone's cupcakes baked, cooled, and frosted by the time the class ended.

It was fifteen minutes past the hour when Mel realized only half the class had appeared.

"Angie, did anyone call out from tonight's class?" she asked.

"Not that I know of. I'll go check the messages," Angie offered.

Mel glanced up to find Emily and Claire watching her with pity in her eyes.

"What?" she asked.

"Nothing," Claire said as she sent Emily a look that clearly said "Shut up."

"You may as well tell me," Mel said. "I'm going to find out sooner or later."

She saw her other three students watching, and she
sighed. She had a feeling she was not going to like this.

"No messages," Angie announced as she came back to
the kitchen.

"Spill it," Mel said to Emily.

"They're not coming," she said. She pressed her lips together as if she wished she never had to utter the words.

"Don't tell me, let me guess," Mel said. "They think I'm
a murderer."

"We told them it wasn't true," Claire said.

"We saw Barbara and Cheryl at Sprouts, in the bulk
food section, and they said they weren't coming, and neither were Marlo, Pat, or Bianca," Emily said. "We should
have told you."

"But we thought they'd change their minds," Claire explained. "That newspaper article read like a tabloid, all in-
nuendo and no fact, but obviously they believed it."

"Idiots," Emily said with a sniff.

Mel glanced at her other three students. "You don't believe the article?"

"No," they said together.

Mildred, the oldest student by far at eighty-two years of
age, shook her head. "You're from South Scottsdale, dear,
you're one of us. If you did kill that girl, I'm sure you had
your reasons."

Mel wasn't sure whether she wanted to hug her or throt-
tle her. She chose to hug her.

"Thanks," she said as she enveloped Mildred in a loose-
armed squeeze. "I appreciate that. I didn't do it, but I appreciate your support all the same."

She directed her students back to work, and when everyone was busy, she sidled up to Angie.

"You know what this means," she said.

"If students drop out of class because of the bad press,
then our customers may go the same way."

"Yeah," Mel said.

"At least sixty percent of our customers are tourists," Angie noted. "They're not going to know about the Christie situation."

"Yes, but most of those customers buy one to four cupcakes maximum," Mel said. "It's our locals who order dozens for parties and weddings. Without that income, I don't know if we can stay afloat."

Angie mirrored her frown. "So, what do we do?"

"Find out who killed Christie," Mel said. "Before our cupcakes are sunk."

Eleven

Once class was dismissed, Mel locked up the bakery, gave Angie a bracing hug, and trotted up the stairs to her apartment.

She decided to skip dinner; it was late, and anxiety about losing her business was making her stomach roll. There wasn't much she could eat that would soothe her nerves right now. She made herself a mug of ginger tea and grabbed her cordless phone.

Instead of tracking Phoebe on the Internet as she had Alma, she decided to call Alma and ask her for Phoebe's information directly. She hoped that Alma could give her a heads-up on how to approach Phoebe.

Alma answered on the third ring. "What?"

"It's Melanie Cooper."

"I know, I have caller ID. What do you want?"

Mel was surprised she'd even picked up.

"How'd the job interview go?"

"Really?" Alma asked. "Is that what you wanted to ask me, or are you being polite?"

"Polite."

"Don't waste our collective time," Alma said.

"Okay, then, how can I get in touch with Phoebe?"

There was a pause on the other end.

"Same way you contacted me," Alma said.

"Or you could save me an hour and give me her information."

"Why have you waited this long to contact her?" Alma asked. "I'd have thought you'd talk to her right after talking to me."

"She seemed really upset," Mel said. "I wanted to give her some time."

"Yeah, she had a real worship thing going for Christie. It's sort of ironic."

"Ironic how?" Mel asked.

"Phoebe was way more talented than Christie. In fact, every award Christie won was because of Phoebe. She gave her all of her best designs and never held anything back."

"Whereas you . . ."

"Kept my best work in a vault where Christie couldn't get to it," Alma said. "I wanted to have a future when I was released from my contract."

"Do you think Phoebe'd be willing to talk to me?"

"Hard to say," Alma said. "She's pretty torn up about Christie, and she knows you're a suspect. She might not want to have anything to do with you."

"Encouraging."

"I'm just saying."

Alma read off Phoebe's phone number while Mel scribbled the information on the back of an empty envelope she found on her desk.

"Thanks, Alma."

"Don't mention it."

Mel knew she was probably feeling oversensitive with half of her class not showing up because they thought she

was a murderer, but still, Alma's tone had sounded omi-
nously like a threat.

Undaunted, she dialed the number, hoping to catch
Phoebe before she went to bed. She waited through two
rings before a very faint voice answered.

"Hello?"

"Hi, Phoebe, it's Melanie Cooper from Fairy Tale Cupcakes."

Mel heard a gasp. Hard to know what to say to that,
so she forged ahead as if it hadn't sounded like Phoebe
had just fainted. "I was wondering if I could ask you a few
questions."

There was a pause, and then Phoebe's meek voice asked,
"Why?"

"Well, the police seem to think I have a strong motive
for murdering Christie," Mel said. "But I didn't do it, and I
need to find out who did."

There was another beat of silence, and Mel wondered if
Phoebe had hung up on her. She knew she would if a person she thought was a murderer called her to chat.

"What do you want to know?"

"Was Christie fighting with anyone? Was she having
personal or business problems that you know of?"

"The police already asked me all of this," Phoebe said
with a weary sigh. "I'm really not up to talking about it. I
can't imagine why anyone would hurt Christie, she was a
goddess."

Huh? Mel felt bad that Christie was dead, no question,
but how could Alma and Phoebe view the same woman so
differently? And given what Alma had said about Phoebe's
talent, why would she put up with a woman who ripped
her off?

"Alma doesn't seem to see her the same way you do,"
Mel said.

"You've talked to Alma?" Phoebe asked, but didn't wait

for her answer. "Of course you have. Alma is, how can I say this, bitter?"

"Bitter, how?" Mel asked. She wanted to hear Phoebe admit that Christie was taking credit for their work.

"She never really committed to be part of the studio," Phoebe said. "She acted as if her designs belonged to her and not the company, which is ridiculous. Our work embodied the ideals of the Christie Stevens Design Studio. When it won awards, we won awards. And it was Christie's ambition and drive that made sure we won."

Phoebe's voice broke, and Mel heard her suck in a gasp of air. "I'm sorry, I just can't imagine what will happen to me without her."

"I'm so sorry for your loss," Mel said.

"Are you?" Phoebe asked.

"Excuse me?" Mel asked.

"I know what the police think," she said. "They think you poisoned her with a cupcake so you could have Tate Harper for yourself."

Mel felt her heart thud in her chest. How did Phoebe know what the police thought?

As if she'd read her mind, Phoebe continued, "I've been spending a lot of time with Christie's family. They're very distraught. Christie's father has brought in a private toxicologist and has been pressuring the Scottsdale Police Department to make an arrest. It should happen any day now."

Uncle Stan hadn't told her any of this when he interviewed Angie earlier in the day. Mel wondered if he even knew what the Stevens family was doing. She felt her insides squeeze tight, as if clenched by a fist. Not that she thought for a second that her uncle would do anything out of bounds to help her, but still it was comforting to have an ally on the force, unless he was being kept out of the loop because of her.

"I haven't heard about any of this . . ." Mel stammered.

"I only took your call because I wanted to tell you that if you're the one who harmed Christie, I'll see you rotting behind bars if it's the last thing I do."

Phoebe's voice broke on a sob and she slammed the phone down. Ouch!

Mel put her phone back in its cradle. Well, that hadn't accomplished much, except to establish the fact that she was in the sights of the Scottsdale PD and the ick that was surrounding her was now leaking onto anyone else in her vicinity, like Tate and Angie and probably Uncle Stan.

She had to find someone else to step up and wear the crown of chief suspect. A thought niggled the back of her mind. What about Christie's rival? If anyone wanted Christie gone, wouldn't it be her competition? Had anyone looked closely at Terry Longmore, or had they just embraced the idea of a love triangle and looked no further?

Mel fired up her laptop to see if Longmore Designs had a Web page. Sure enough. Two links into Google and she hit pay dirt. Stick figure models faded in and out on the home page, wearing a lot of black eyeliner, faux fur, and platforms. Ew.

Under the "about" tab, Mel clicked and saw a brief bio on Terry Longmore and her two top designers. Interesting. Maybe claiming your protégé's work as your own wasn't the norm.

She jotted down the address and phone. The Longmore Studio was located in downtown Phoenix, nowhere near Christie's studio. Interesting. Mel decided to call Terry Longmore tomorrow and see what she had to say about Christie Stevens.

In her petite bathroom, she studied her face in the mirror. She remembered Joe saying that her haircut made her eyes look big, and she wondered again if it was in a good way or a bad way.

Whatever. She brushed her teeth, refusing to think about him and his date, or the fact that she hadn't yet repainted the walls her mother had done in mango.

No, it was much better to think about Tate's loss and the fact that she was the prime suspect for murder, which was beginning to have seriously adverse effects upon her business. Mel unfolded her futon and rolled out her sheets and blanket.

She expected sleep would be a long time in coming, but she was asleep before she finished a jaw-popping yawn.

\'`\'`\

"We're low on Blonde Bombshells, Tinkerbells, and Death by Chocolates," Angie hollered from inside the walk-in.

Mel noted the three flavors on the pad in front of her. "Got it."

This was good. She would have a nice morning baking her butt off, and could pretend that everything was business as usual for at least a little while.

Angie closed the door to the walk-in behind her and sat on the stool beside Mel's.

"I tried calling Tate last night," she said. "He never answered or called me back."

A worried V perched between Angie's eyebrows, and Mel reached over and patted her hand.

"He's got a lot going on," she said. "He'll come around when he's ready."

"He didn't answer your messages either, did he?"

"No," Mel admitted.

"Well, I've had it," Angie said. "We're his friends, and he needs us. I'm going over there today, and he's going to talk to me if I have to hold his head over the toilet bowl and threaten him with a swirly."

Mel grinned. She could just picture it.

"Who's getting a swirly?" a voice asked from the door.

It was Tate. He looked haggard and worn, like he'd been backed over by a dump truck, repeatedly. Both Angie and Mel hopped up from their stools and ran across the room to hug him.

He was wearing jeans and a rumpled, long-sleeved T-shirt. His arms locked around both of them, and he hauled them close.

" 'Honest men stay honest only as long as it pays. That's why I'm a thief and you're a liar.' " Tate let them go.

"Jack Strawhorn in *Posse*," Angie said. "Who's a liar?" Tate looked away.

"What's going on, Tate?" Mel asked.

He paced across the kitchen. The same kitchen he had spent a month of Saturdays in, helping to clean, paint, and stock with supplies. He fingered the door to the walk-in pantry full of dry goods as if he wished he could lock himself up in there as well.

Angie opened her mouth to press him, but Mel put her hand on her elbow to hold her in check. Angie gave her a curt nod and clamped her lips together.

"I always thought when I asked a woman to marry me, it would be the happiest moment of my life," he said.

Mel and Angie exchanged glances. Where was this going?

Tate faced them, his boyish features giving them a rueful smile. "I was wrong."

"What's going on, Tate?" Angie asked.

"I don't remember asking Christie to marry me," he said.

"What do you mean?" Mel asked. "Did you block it out?"

"No, I mean, I don't remember it. Period."

He resumed pacing, and passed a hand through his thick

brown hair. His face was pinched with stress, making him appear older than his thirty-four years.

"We went to dinner, and she started talking about marriage," he said. "I remember thinking, whoa, as we'd only been dating a few months, but she was so happy, I said nothing. We had a few more drinks and then took a walk along the canal. The rest of the night is blurry, but I vaguely remember being in a jewelry store. When we woke up the next morning, she had a ring on her finger and a date in mind."

"Wait, let me get this straight," Angie said. Her expression was a mixture of confusion and hopefulness. "You didn't ask her to marry you?"

"But she had a ring on," he said. "I must have asked her, right?"

"Oh, my God!" Angie clapped a hand over her mouth. Then she slowly lowered it and said, "I bet she drugged you."

Tate looked pained, and Mel knew the thought had crossed his mind as well.

"Why didn't you tell us this before?" she asked.

"I couldn't be sure," he said. "But since her death, I'm finding out more and more about how she treated people and how she got what she wanted, and it's not—pleasant."

"That miserable . . ." Angie spluttered, but Tate cut her off. "No, Ange, no matter what she did, she didn't deserve what happened to her."

Angie looked as if she would have argued, but obviously thought better of it.

"I talked to Phoebe last night," Mel said. "She said that Christie's father has hired his own forensics people and is pushing the police department hard for an arrest."

"It's true," Tate agreed. "He and I had a bit of a blowout yesterday."

He picked up one of Mel's cupcake-shaped pot holders and squeezed it in his fist like it was a stress release ball.

She had a feeling it was keeping him from putting his fist through the wall.

A knock on the door frame interrupted whatever Tate had been about to say.

Detective Rayburn was standing there with a folded paper in his hand. Behind him, Mel saw several uniformed Scottsdale police officers in their distinctive khaki uniforms. What struck her as odd was that they all wore blue latex gloves. In a free-falling swoop, she felt her stomach drop to her toes.

"Hello, Detective," she said.

He glanced between her and Tate. She didn't like the speculative light in his eyes.

"Is Uncle Stan with you?" she asked.

"No, but I have a warrant to search the premises," he said. "Both here and the apartment above."

Mel took the piece of paper he offered between stiff fingers.

"I don't understand," she said. "Where is Uncle Stan?"

He gave her an annoyed glance. "He's been removed from the case."

"What?" Angie snapped. "Why?"

"Probably you should ask your brother in the DA's office about that," Rayburn snapped.

"Don't move," Angie said. "I'm calling Joe."

Another detective stepped forward. He was a middle-aged Hispanic man with gray hair at his temples and wearing glasses. He extended his hand to Tate.

"I'm Detective Gonzales," he said. "You're Tate Harper?"

"Yes," Tate said. His eyes looked wary, and Mel knew he felt just as hunted as she did.

"I'd like you to come to my office so I can ask you some questions."

Mel gasped. She didn't mean to, it just slipped out. Tate gave her shoulder a reassuring squeeze.

"Certainly," Tate said. He took his cell phone out of his pocket and hit a button. "I'll just let my attorney know, so he can join us."

Mel felt her eyebrows lift up to her hairline. Tate lifted the phone to his ear and barked a few words into it. His gaze was sharp as he studied the detective, and he drew himself up to his full height, so that he looked down on the man. This was corporate Tate, the businessman, not her Groucho Marx-quoting buddy.

"I'll be back as soon as it's finished," he said to Mel. She watched as the two men exited the kitchen.

She turned around and saw the uniformed officers with the gloves searching through her pantry. When one of them shoved his gloved hand into the large bin of flour and dumped a fistful of it into a clear plastic bag, she felt her temper begin to get the better of her.

"Detective," she said, "these are my supplies. I can't have people's hands being shoved into my dry goods."

She cringed when another officer did the same with her sugar.

"I'm sorry, ma'am," Rayburn said. "That warrant gives us the right to search anything we deem necessary."

Mel opened the legal document. Her eyes saw the state and county names printed in bold at the top and the search warrant number listed below. She tried to read the legal speak, but given her increasing state of panic, it was like gibberish to her.

Angie came out of the office with a slam of the door. Her face was bright red, and Mel suspected that she hadn't been talking to Joe so much as yelling at him.

"Come on," she said. She grabbed Mel's elbow and led her out front.

"I really think we should stay," Mel said. She didn't like turning the kitchen over, unsupervised, even to law enforcement personnel.

"There's nothing we can do," Angie said.

When they stepped out the front door, Mel was shocked to see a small gathering of tourists. The police cars took up all the parking spots in front of her building, and she knew it looked bad.

Murmurs started, and Mel felt panic begin to spread like a virus inside her. All they needed now was a news van to roll by, and their business would be finished.

She glanced up and down the street. Diagonally across from them sat a big pink van. Olivia was watching them, leaning against the back end with a wide smile on her face. Mel wished she had her bowl of frosting now. Only this time she wouldn't be aiming for the van.

She had to do something to save the situation. Two more officers passed her to go into the bakery.

An older gentleman with a walker peered past Mel into the shop. He pushed back the cowboy hat perched on his head and said, "Who's the party for?"

Mel could have kissed him.

In as loud a voice as she could muster, she said, "That's right. Fairy Tale Cupcakes is hosting a private party for the Scottsdale PD. We're sorry for the inconvenience, but since it's a surprise party, we need everyone to clear the way, so the guest of honor doesn't suspect."

She saw a few people exchange smiles and nods, and one woman said, "Great idea. I think I'll do that for my granddaughter's birthday party. Can I call you?"

"Absolutely," Angie said. She reached into her apron and handed the woman one of their cupcake-shaped business cards.

As the crowd dispersed and Olivia drove off in a huff, Mel and Angie took seats at one of the small café tables in front of the store for people who wanted to enjoy their cupcakes outside.

Mel glanced up and down the street at the western-looking buildings with false square fronts. Everything seemed normal; even the old stagecoach was hitched to its two horses, ready to take tourists around the block, but it all felt surreal, as if she were out of step with the world around her.

"Quick thinking," Angie said.

"Thanks," Mel replied. "Good thing you dragged me out here, so we could head off a disaster."

"This is so wrong," Angie fumed. "How can they possibly think that you'd do anything to hurt Christie?"

"It gets worse," Mel said. "A Detective Gonzales asked Tate to come in for questioning."

"When did this happen?" Angie asked.

"While you were on the phone. Sorry."

"Was Tate okay?"

"He was a pro," Mel said. "He let his inner corporate muckety-muck take over."

"Excellent," Angie said. "Now, listen, I talked to Joe."

"Please tell me there's good news here."

"It depends upon your point of view," Angie said.

"I'm pretty much at the place where not only is the glass half-empty, but someone dropped it on the floor and smashed it, but I'll try."

"Joe's the one who had Uncle Stan removed from the case."

"What? Why?"

"Joe thought it would hurt both you and Uncle Stan if your relationship became public, which he's convinced it would," Angie replied. "Also, he's trying to protect you both from any hint of impropriety, so the Stevens family won't have cause to hit you with a civil suit later on."

"Humph." Mel knew Joe was probably right, but still, it grated. She felt protected when Uncle Stan was on the case, but now she was at the mercy of Rayburn. "Did Joe say anything else?"

"Only that the investigation is ongoing," Angie said. "I asked if they knew the cause of death and he said he couldn't say, but that he hadn't heard anything definitive from the medical examiner yet."

"Is that good or bad?"

Angie shrugged. "I'd have to say bad. If they could figure out what killed her, they could zero in on a suspect. Without a cause of death, it leaves it wide open and keeps you and Tate as the main suspects."

"There has to be someone else," Mel said. "What about some of the other wedding vendors?"

"Or that other designer that Alma mentioned."

"Terry Longmore. I'm on that one already," Mel said. "As soon as Tate is free, let's see if he can give us any more names."

"In the meantime?" Angie asked.

"Business as usual," Mel said.

"For as long as it lasts," Angie said with a sigh.

Twelve

Several hours passed before Detective Rayburn and his crew departed. Mel and Angie had waited, sitting in a booth inside the shop. Angie had begun to make a list of all the items that would need replacing when the officers left.

Mel felt as if she were in suspended animation. She didn't want to hover and draw attention to herself, but she didn't know what to do either. She debated calling her mother and having her call the attorney Johnny Dietz had recommended, but she hesitated. Mostly because she didn't want to appear guilty. But did it really matter when everyone seemed to think she was guilty?

When the detectives left, she sagged with relief, mostly because they hadn't handcuffed her and dragged her with them.

Angie had just locked the door behind them when Tate entered through the door to the kitchen. He looked grim.

"We need to talk," he said.

"Not here." Mel didn't really think the detectives had

bugged the bakery, but she had watched a few too many
episodes of *24*, and couldn't help but think that Jack Bauer
would never risk it.

"What . . ." Angie began, but Mel cut her off by putting
a finger over her lips.

She gestured for them to follow her, and the three of
them headed out the back door. Mel locked it behind them
and led the way down the alley, across Brown Street, and
into Civic Center Park. She stopped beside a fountain that
sprayed in a large bubble, and hoped the noise would keep
their conversation from being overheard.

"What do you know?" Mel asked Tate.

"There was arsenic in the cupcake."

"That's impossible!" Angie said.

They were standing huddled in a small circle. The sun
was setting, and it would soon be dark. The evening hadn't
cooled off yet, but Mel felt a chill walk across her skin with
icy fingers.

"So that's why they were searching the bakery," Mel
said. "To see if I had arsenic mixed in with my chocolate
chips."

"It gets more interesting than that." Tate leaned closer.
"My attorney has connections at the police department and
at the medical examiner's office. Get this: The initial autopsy showed no trace of arsenic in the contents of Christie's stomach."

"What does that mean?" Angie asked.

"It means it wasn't arsenic that killed her," Tate said.

"Then why are they searching my bakery?" Mel asked.

"Because something killed her, but they have no idea
what," Tate said. "It may or may not have been in the
cupcakes."

"Someone tampered with my cupcakes," Mel said. She
thought back to Alma and her five-year contract. There

was a lot of anger there, and Alma certainly had motive and opportunity.

"It could be anyone," Angie stated. "Tate, do you know who was at the photo shoot? And who Christie was dealing with for the wedding? Did she lock anyone else into a contract they were unhappy about?"

"She had a big fight with Jay Driscoll, the photographer, the day of the shoot. He's high fashion and she used him for a lot of her layouts, but he was balking about doing our wedding. He didn't like her having ownership of the pictures."

"I know how he felt," Mel muttered.

"You should have come to me," Tate said. "I would never have made you sign over ownership of your cupcakes."

Mel could see the hurt in his eyes. He was right. She should have gone to him, and then they wouldn't be in this mess.

"Just like you should have told us that you didn't remember proposing to Christie," Angie snapped.

"Point taken," Tate admitted. Angie looked somewhat mollified.

"So, what's the plan?" Angie asked, looking between them.

"I'm going to keep doing what I've been doing," Mel said. "I'm going to keep talking to people. And next on my list are Jay Driscoll and Terry Longmore."

"The designer?" Angie asked.

"Yes, she and Christie had a rivalry that was apparently quite intense," Mel said. "I'm going to drop by her design studio and see what I can find out."

A small smile played on Tate's lips.

"What?" Mel asked.

" 'I just find it hard to believe that you're a man,' " Tate quoted.

" 'Because you found me attractive as a woman?' " Angie finished.

"Okay, what's with the *Victor/Victoria* references?" Mel asked. They stared at her until she got it. "Oh, Terry Longmore is a man."

"Who dresses like a woman," Tate said.

"Maybe I'll start with the photographer," Mel decided.

✄ ✄ ✄

Jay Driscoll had a studio on the outskirts of the artsy section of Old Town Scottsdale, on Fifth Avenue between a pet groomer and a guitar store.

Mel propped her Schwinn Cruiser bicycle against the side of the building and locked it to the handrail that led up the short staircase. She had been thinking of how she would approach the photographer. Obviously, she wanted to know how he had felt about Christie, but how was she going to get him to confide in her?

She'd just have to wing it. She pulled open the door and stepped inside. Like Christie's studio, this one was a study in minimalism with white walls, a black granite reception desk, and no chairs. Obviously, lingering was not encouraged here.

"Hello?" she called. Her voice echoed in the cavernous space, and she had a brutal flashback to the morning she found Christie's body.

She glanced nervously around the main room. Huge black-and-white portraits of models in haute couture covered the walls. She glanced nervously across the brown concrete floor. There was no sign of a body.

She felt a coating of sweat bead up under her long-sleeved T-shirt, and she pushed the sleeves up to her elbows, more to give herself something to do than to relieve her sudden case of the sweats.

"Marlena!" a voice called from behind a frosted glass wall, and Mel felt her shoulders drop in relief. "Marlena!"

Footsteps echoed on the hard floor as a man dressed all in black pushed open a red door in the frosted glass wall and stepped into the room. He was spider thin, wearing black cowboy boots, skinny black jeans, and a black silk dress shirt that was untucked. His hair was thick and gray, and styled in a wispy way that reminded Mel of Richard Avedon. He had a large, clunky camera hanging from a strap around his neck. Jay Driscoll.

His gaze raked Mel from head to toe. "You're not Marlena."

"No, I'm Melanie Cooper," she said and extended her hand. He ignored it. "I was hoping to speak with you, Mr. Driscoll."

He let out a put-upon sigh. "Let me save us both some time. You're tall, but you're too heavy to be a runway model. What are you? A size eight or a ten? I can't work with anything over a four. And, frankly, although the boyish hairdo does fabulous things for your eyes, you're too ordinary-looking to be a print model. Pretty, yes, but ordinary. You really need to have fuller lips or a needle-thin nose—you know, something that makes you look exotic. And besides, aren't you a little old to want to be a model?"

Mel felt her jaw drop. Was this guy for real? He looked past her as if the missing Marlena might be hiding behind her. She resisted the urge to kick him in his shapeless backside, barely.

"Actually, I have no interest in being a model, but thanks for the blow to my self-esteem. Really, I appreciate it," she said.

He shrugged as if to say "whatever," and asked, "Then why are you here?"

"I came to ask you some questions about Christie Stevens."

That got his attention. He looked at her again, but now he was wary.

"Who are you?"

"Melanie Cooper."

"Are you a cop?"

"No," she said. "Just a friend."

"Well, I have nothing to tell you. I already spoke to the police. I don't know anything about what happened to her that night. When I left the studio, she was fine."

"What time did you leave?" Mel asked.

"Just before midnight," he said. "My assistant, Marlena, was with me."

"Did you see any cupcakes at the photo shoot?" Mel asked.

"Cupcakes? No, I never eat those things," he said. "They're all fat and sugar, death in a paper cup. Why are you asking me about cupcakes?"

He looked at her as if she were deranged, and then a light flickered in his pale gray eyes.

"It's you," he said. "The cupcake killer."

"The what?" Mel asked. "I am not!"

"I read about you in the paper," he said. He lifted his camera and stared at her through the lens. "You're the childhood friend of the groom, who wanted him back so desperately that you poisoned the cupcakes you were hired to bake for the wedding, and killed her."

"I did not!" Mel protested. She covered her head with her arms and turned away to keep him from getting a good picture.

"Stand still," he ordered. "A good picture of you could net me a small fortune."

"From high fashion to paparazzi, is that how you want your career to go?" Mel asked.

The room became silent, and she glanced over her

shoulder. Jay Driscoll lowered his camera with a look of self-loathing on his face.

"Were you booked to take Christie's wedding photos?" she asked before he reconsidered.

"Yeah," he said. He didn't sound happy about it.

Mel knew she was going to have to pretend to be empathetic in order to gain his trust. Although at the moment, she felt that Christie and Jay were a match made in egocentric heaven.

"Look, I'm asking questions because the police think I had something to do with her death. I didn't."

He studied her through narrowed eyes, but Mel couldn't tell if he believed her or not.

"She asked me to sign a contract giving her ownership of the cupcakes I designed for her wedding, which I was very unhappy with," Mel said. "I mean, to sign over my own creations . . ."

"Exactly!" Jay snapped his fingers. "I tried to explain to her that the photographer retains the rights to wedding photos, but she was having none of it."

"Did you consider refusing her?" Mel asked.

"I started to . . ."

He paced away from her to stand in front of a life-sized print of a model, looking very Audrey Hepburn in a chemise dress and big hat, on the streets of what Mel recognized as Paris.

"Lately, my career has been subdued," he said.

Mel figured that was a euphemism for "in a nosedive."

"The magazines are looking for younger photographers because they think they're more innovative. Ha! They have no appreciation for the history of fashion."

Mel was quiet, hoping he would continue. He turned back to face her, and he looked uncertain, almost afraid.

"If I'm not Jay Driscoll, fashion photographer, then who

am I? Christie knew I'd been passed over for several large shoots, and my agent said I desperately needed the publicity to get back in the game."

He ran a well-manicured hand through his wispy hair, making it stand on end even more.

"I begged Christie to let me retain copyright of at least a few of the photos to put on display or use in my portfolio. She laughed at me and refused. In the end, I had to agree to her terms and hope she placed them in a magazine of note and gave me the credit."

"Your agent was okay with this?" Mel asked.

"Desperate times," he said with a small smile.

Mel still didn't like him very much, but she did feel for him. He had been in an untenable position, much like her own. Obviously, however, Christie's murder was not to his advantage, because now he didn't even have the hope that his photos might garner him some attention.

Hmm. She would have preferred to keep him on her suspect list, but it just didn't seem likely, unless, of course, it had been a crime of passion. She tried to picture Christie and Jay together, but couldn't quite manage it.

The front door opened and in sashayed a young woman, no more than twenty-two, Mel would have guessed. She wore a bright yellow sarong-style dress that enhanced the deep coffee color of her skin and her waist-length black hair. She had the requisite full lips of a wannabe model and a brilliant white smile.

"Ah, Marlena," Jay said, and opened his arms. The girl entwined herself around the man old enough to be her grandfather, and Mel felt any sympathy she'd built for Jay Driscoll evaporate like dew on a hot summer morning.

"This is Melanie Cooper, the cupcake killer," he said.

Marlena looked at Mel with wide eyes.

"Not really," Mel said. "I just happened to be the one to find the body."

"It wasn't surprising that someone harmed her," Marlena said in a charming French accent. "She was not right in her mind, and neither were her assistants."

"True," Jay agreed. "Do you remember that crazy scene about the weight-loss patch?"

Marlena nodded.

Jay looked at Mel and said, "In the middle of the shoot, she and her assistant left for what was it, a half hour, to go put on some crazy appetite suppressant patch.

"We'd ordered in pizzas from Oreganos, and they were terrified that they'd eat too much if they didn't control it. The whole shoot ground to a halt because Christie wouldn't let me take a picture without her approval. It was mental."

Which certainly sounded like the Christie Mel had come to know. The question was who had been driven to murder by the high-maintenance bride-to-be?

Jay must have read her thoughts, because he looked directly at her and said, "It wasn't me."

His stare was unblinking, but Mel wasn't quite sure she believed him.

Thirteen

"That's it!" Angie declared. "Do you have any idea how lucky you are that Driscoll didn't snap your picture and sell it for big bucks? You're too well known now. You have to let me help you."

"Yeah, I know," Mel said, and blew out a breath. They were sitting at the steel table in the kitchen, enjoying a quick coffee break between customers.

"It's not just about you being a suspect anymore," Angie continued. "This is *our* business that we stand to lose. Besides, Tate is my friend, too, and I want to help."

"Okay," Mel said.

"I mean, I have skills," Angie said. "I can ask questions, and believe you me, I can get answers."

"You're in."

"I—what?" Angie asked.

Mel laughed. "I need you to pretend to be a very wealthy bride-to-be. Are you up to it?"

"Are you kidding?" Angie rose from her seat and pretended to have a bouquet in hand while walking like a bride down the aisle and singing, "Da-da-da-dum."

Mel laughed. This might just work.

✓⸍*✓*⸌

Terry Longmore Designs was located in downtown Phoenix in an industrial warehouse off Seventh Street, south of the Interstate. There was plenty of parking around the building, which looked like it had been hit by every single tagger in the metro area. Mel studied the vivid graffiti and noticed the initials T, L, and D were worked into the loops and swirls of the neon spray paint. Very hip.

Her phone vibrated, and she flipped it open. "Hello."

"Passing you," Angie said.

Mel glanced up and saw Angie drive by in her red Mini Cooper. They had switched cars, thinking that Angie's white Honda would be less noticeable, and given that Mel was going to be sitting outside the building in it, she was all about not being noticed.

"Remember to leave your phone on in the outside pocket of your purse," Mel said as she watched Angie park and climb out of the car. "That way I can hear your conversation."

"Got it," Angie said.

She had dressed the part of the ingenuc bride. She let her long black hair tumble down her back in thick waves. With her mother's four-carat emerald cocktail ring on her left hand and a gray organdy over yellow cotton dress, designed by Yoana Baraschi and borrowed from Angie's sister-in-law, she looked every inch the wealthy young woman shopping for her wedding gown.

They had called Terry Longmore yesterday and arranged a meeting. The plan was for Angie to work Christie into the conversation and see how Terry reacted. Mel wanted to know if he had a motive for killing off his competition. If he acted suspicious, Mel and Angie had agreed that Angie should leave immediately.

Sitting outside the large block of concrete and steel, Mel wondered if she should have gone in with Angie or, even crazier, sent her mother.

She lifted her field glasses and watched as Angie approached the bright orange door to the right of several steel garage doors. She pressed the doorbell, and Mel heard an annoying buzzing sound come from her phone. Well, at least the phones were working.

"Who is it?" a voice asked from the intercom.

Angie pressed the Talk button and answered, "Angie DeLaura."

"Oh, you're punctual,. How very Miss Manners of you."

The door in front of her unlocked with a click, and Angie pulled it open and stepped inside.

Mel lowered the glasses. She hated that she couldn't see Angie. It made her nervous. Not that she thought Terry would harm Angie, but what if he was the killer? What if he figured out what they were up to? Angie could be in danger. Mel lifted her phone and was about to yell, "Abort! Abort!" when she heard Angie talking.

"Nice to meet you, Mr. Longmore," she said. *"Don't take this the wrong way, but you look like you'd be more comfortable working on cars than clothes."*

A deep laugh echoed out of Mel's phone, followed by a pleasant male voice. *"Don't let the ripped jeans and Nascar T-shirt fool you. I design a hell of a wedding dress. However, you probably expected to see me in a ball gown and tiara,"* he guessed.

"Er . . . more like a spangled halter with fishnets and stilettos," Angie said.

He laughed again. *"I'll have to keep that in mind for the next time we meet."*

Mel felt herself smiling as she listened. Terry Longmore certainly had charm.

It was silent for a moment, and then Mel heard him say, *"Contrary to popular opinion, I'm not really a cross-dresser."*

"Then why . . . ?" Angie's voice trailed off as if she was unsure of how to phrase her question.

"Why does everyone think I am?" he finished for her.

Mel found herself leaning closer, wanting to hear his answer.

"When I first started designing, I did primarily men's clothes. But frankly, it's boring. You never get to play with fuchsia satin if you're creating for men. So, I started playing with women's wear."

Mel heard the sound of footsteps, and assumed they were walking while Terry continued talking.

"I became so caught up in the creations, I forgot about comfort, and during a disastrous photo shoot, one of my models challenged me to wear my own design."

She heard Angie giggle, and she looked at the phone as if it had hiccupped. Angie didn't giggle.

"I took the challenge and discovered I couldn't walk, couldn't sit, and couldn't pee. Suffice to say, lesson learned. Well, Sadie, the model, thought it was so funny, she called the photographers at Vogue *and had them do a shoot with me in the damn outfit, and after that, we did another shoot in a few of my new comfortable, wearable designs. Since then, I've always made a prototype for myself to test drive, and it's given me a rep as a cross-dresser, which I can live with for all of the free publicity."*

"A friend of mine used to be in marketing," Angie said. *"I believe she would say that was very savvy."*

If Mel didn't know better, she would think Angie was flirting. Nah, it couldn't be. Angie didn't flirt. She was just playing her part really, really well.

"Now, as fascinating as I am," Terry said, *"I'm guessing you're not here to talk about me."*

"Not exactly," Angie agreed. *"As I mentioned on the phone, I'm getting married, and I need a gown."*

"May I say, he is a very, very lucky man," Terry said.

"Oh, thank you," Angie simpered.

Angie sounded flustered, and Mel wondered if she was blushing. This was not at all how she had envisioned this going. She could hear the clatter of dishes, and then heard Terry's voice again.

"Would you like sugar in your coffee, although I doubt a girl as sweet as you would even need it?" he said.

Oh, good grief! Mel was pretty sure she was going to throw up. Angie giggled again, and Mel thought it might be time for an intervention.

"I have a confession to make,"

Mel pressed the phone closer to her ear.

"I was going to hire Christie Stevens to design my gown."

"Were you?" Terry asked. *"How unfortunate for you that she suffered such a tragedy."*

Even through the phone, Mel could tell he thought it was anything but.

"It has set me back a bit," Angie said. *"Although I'm not sure I was happy with her."*

"Really? In what way?"

"She was, well, mean," Angie said. *"She told me I had to lose ten pounds if I wanted to look good in her design."*

"No!"

"Yes!" Angie said with just the right amount of indignant hurt.

Go, girl! Mel thought. *Reel him in.*

"*Angie, I'm going to be blunt,*" Terry said. "*Christie was a bitch.*"

The venom in his voice dripped through the phone, and Mel thought perhaps he did have a motive to kill Christie, if hatred was a motive.

"*Sorry,*" he said. "*That came out a little harsh.*"

"*It's okay,*" Angie said. "*I happen to agree with you. I imagine she must have made your life very difficult, being in the same business and all.*"

There was a pause, as if he was considering what she said and how to respond.

"*You have no idea,*" he said. "*Between you and me, the police have been here three times. Just because we were business rivals, they think I might have had something to do with her death.*"

"*No!*"

"*Ridiculous, isn't it?*" he asked.

Mel was thinking *not so much,* and she wondered if Angie was thinking the same.

"*I heard the police suspect her fiancé and his child-hood friend,*" Angie said in a stage whisper.

"*I suppose it's possible,*" Terry said.

"*But you don't think it's likely?*" Angie asked.

"*I don't know,*" he said. "*I've met her fiancé at some events and he seemed nice, too nice for her.*"

"*Do you know anyone else who wanted to harm her?*" she asked.

"*Try everyone who ever had to do business with her. She used people up like they were Kleenex, completely disposable.*"

"*Including her designers,*" Angie said.

"*Yeah, I wasn't going to mention it, but from what I've heard, she was a nightmare to work for. I try to give my people the credit they deserve. I've got fresh grads from*

*the Rhode Island School of Design here. I know they're
not planning to be with me forever. I don't lock them
into untenable contracts. They're allowed to shine with
their own designs. Christie didn't do that. She suffocated
people."*

"Until someone suffocated her," Angie said. "Or something like that."

"You reap what you sow."

"Indeed. But your business must be reaping some ben-
efits from her demise," Angie suggested.

Mel held her breath. Angie was going for the jugular.
How would Terry respond?

A pair of hairy knuckles rapped on Mel's window, making her jump and drop her phone. It fell to the floor and
slammed shut. No! Her connection to Angie was cut off.

She glared out the window. There, attached to the hairy
knuckles, stood two of Angie's older brothers, Sal and
Tony. She lowered the window.

"Well, isn't this a surprise?" she asked.

Sal frowned at her from under his bushy unibrow.

"Good to see you, Mel," he said. He leaned in and kissed
her cheek, and she was about knocked out by the heady
scent of Brut cologne that surrounded him.

Tony muscled him aside and leaned in to kiss her other
cheek. "Yeah, good to see you."

"You two, too," Mel said.

They stared at her as if waiting for her to make a full
confession. Mel was not about to do so. Instead she just
sat. She tapped the steering wheel and looked at a hermit
warbler sitting on a nearby oleander.

"Well," Sal said. He spread his hands wide. "We're
waiting for an explanation."

"Of what?" Mel asked.

"Why you're here," Tony said. He was the tallest of the
DeLaura brothers and the skinniest.

"I heard there was a paper company that does cupcake liners down here, and I'm checking it out," she answered.

"In Angie's car?" Sal asked.

That was the problem with the DeLauras, they were an observant bunch.

"Mine's in the shop," she lied.

"Really?" Tony asked. "Because it looks like it's parked over there in front of that clothing designer's studio."

Nuts! Too late Mel remembered Tony had helped her change a flat on her car a few months ago; of course he recognized it.

"Where is she, Mel?" Sal asked.

"Who?"

They looked at her with the grim inevitability of prison walls.

"What makes you think she's with me?" Mel asked. "I'm her partner, not her keeper."

"We tracked her cell phone using GPS," Sal said. "When your shop was closed this morning and no one could get in touch with her, we ran the search and followed it to this location. So, what is she doing? Or, more accurately, what are the two of you up to?"

"You tracked her?" Mel asked, sure she must have heard him wrong.

"She's our little sister," Sal said, as if this was all the explanation necessary. "We worry."

"You'd better worry, because if she finds out, she's going to . . ." Mel stopped in midsentence. She'd forgotten Angie was still inside asking the tricky questions. How much time had passed? Should she be out by now? What if something had gone terribly wrong?

She scrambled out of the car and hurried toward the building.

"Mel, I don't like that look on your face," Tony said. "What's happening?"

"Angie's pretending to be a bride-to-be shopping for a gown, so we can scope out Christie's competition and see if maybe he had a motive to kill her. That way the police will stop looking at Tate and me, and our business will be saved."

"You mean she's in there with a killer?" Sal shouted.

"No, I mean, I don't know. I was listening to her conversation on my phone until you two came along and scared me," Mel snapped. "But I do think she should be out by now."

Sal and Tony hurried to the door. Sal pulled a small case out of his suit jacket and unzipped it. He jimmied the two locks on the door and then, with a pop, the door swung wide.

Uncle Stan would be so unhappy about this, Mel thought. Before Sal became a car salesman, he and Uncle Stan had quite a shared history, with Sal being naughty and Uncle Stan catching him.

"You wait out here," Tony said. "You'll be safer, plus they might recognize you. Go wait in your car."

"But . . ." Mel began, but Sal cut her off. "No buts."

Sal still had enough of the thug in him that Mel didn't argue. If Angie needed rescuing, there was no one better for the job than her brothers.

She hurried back across the parking lot and hunkered low in the seat of Angie's car. She was just getting crazy restless when she saw one of the garage doors slide open to admit a black SUV. She blinked. Sitting in the driver's seat was Alma Rodriguez.

Fourteen

The air whooshed out of her lungs in a rush that left Mel dizzy. Alma was driving into Terry Longmore's garage. What did that mean?

She glanced at the door. There was no sign of Sal or Tony or Angie. Mel knew she had a split second to make her decision. She didn't hesitate. Very quietly she opened the car door, and hurried to the side of the building and peered around the corner.

The garage door was still open. She hunched low and crept inside, hoping she wasn't spotted. Parked next to the SUV was a small blue Porsche; she knelt down beside it and listened to her heartbeat pound in her ears. She had no idea what she would say if anyone caught her here. That she was looking for a restroom? She didn't think they'd buy it.

A grinding noise sounded, and as she glanced over her shoulder, she saw the daylight behind her shrinking. She was irrevocably shut in.

A door opened, and she heard the sound of footsteps. Judging by the patter, they belonged to more than one person.

"What are you thinking, bringing it here?"

Mel pressed herself closer to the car as she recognized Terry's voice.

"I had to," Alma said. "I can't have it found with me."

Mel wondered what they were talking about. She squatted lower and tried to see beneath the car as she heard them open the back of the SUV.

"Wow," Terry said. "That's amazing. It's not just a gown, it's a work of art."

"I know," Alma said. She sounded grudging in her agreement.

"Does Phoebe suspect?"

"What? That I'm working for you or that I've made off with her creation before the cops impounded it?"

"Either," Terry said.

Mel could hear the rustle of fabric and saw a flash of white beneath the belly of the car.

"No, Phoebe hasn't gotten out of bed since the incident."

"You're calling Christie's murder an incident?"

"Whatever."

Mel heard the strike of a match, and the smell of cigarette smoke wafted toward her.

"Not near the dress," Terry snapped.

"Fine," Alma said, and Mel heard her walk a few steps away. "Now, I've fulfilled my part of the bargain. When do I start work?"

"What's Phoebe going to do for work?" Terry asked.

"Oh, hell no," Alma said. Mel could see her feet pace back and forth, back and forth the length of the car. "I'm not working with her again. If you give her a spot in your studio, I'll tell her you asked me to hijack the dress she designed for Christie's wedding. I'll out you."

"Relax, it was just a thought," Terry said.

"Well, it was a bad one." Mel saw Alma's cigarette hit the cement floor and watched as she ground it out under her boot heel. "That girl may have some design skills, but she is a nutburger without a bun."

"Are you finished?" Terry asked, his voice impatient. "I'm not having a great day. I just had to coddle a delusional bride, whose two crazy brothers showed up after she wasted my whole morning. She's apparently not getting married after all."

Delusional bride? Mel reared up and smacked her head on the side mirror of the sports car. Biting off a string of curses, she squinched her face and hunkered down, hoping they hadn't heard her.

"What was that?" Terry asked Alma. "It sounded like a banging noise."

There was a beat of silence, and Mel was sure they could hear her heart pounding in her chest like a bass drum.

"It's the sound of me kicking you in the peanuts if you even think of signing on Phoebe."

"Lovely," Terry said.

Mel pressed her hand to the throbbing bump on her head as they went up the shallow steps to the door above.

When she heard the door open and shut, she carefully rose from her spot and crept back towards the closed garage door. Luckily, she was able to lift it just enough to squeeze out beneath it.

Sal and Tony were standing beside the Mini Cooper. Angie revved the engine and peeled out of the parking lot, looking as if she wished her brothers were under the wheels. She stopped short in front of Mel.

"Bakery," she barked, and drove off.

Mel looked at Sal and Tony. They looked bewildered and hurt, but Mel didn't have time to listen to their tales of brotherly woe. She gave them a quick wave, climbed into Angie's car, and sped after her.

∿∿∿

Angie was sitting at the steel worktable in the kitchen, staring at a pile of electronic rubble. She held one of her chunky-soled yellow sandals in her hand, and looked like she was going to club the pile of plastic and wires again if it made one false move.

"I think you killed it," Mel said.

"You can't be too sure," Angie retorted. "You never know when a sneaky, interfering brother or two has put a tracking device in your stuff."

"Mmm," Mel hummed in agreement. She didn't want to say anything that might set Angie off.

"Sal and Tony are banned from the bakery," Angie said. "No cupcakes for them. Period."

"Okay," Mel said.

Angie whacked what used to be her cell phone one more time. Then she rose, and with only one shoe on, she limped over to the garbage can. She brought it back to the table and swept the remnants of her phone into it.

"Better now?" Mel asked.

Angie nodded.

"So, what happened? I lost contact with you when you asked him if his business was getting better with Christie's murder."

"You lost me?" Angie asked. "How?"

Mel didn't say anything, and Angie glowered.

"Never mind, I have a pretty good idea," she huffed.

"Bigger picture, here, Angie," Mel said. "What happened?"

Sprinkle with Murder   147

Angie shook her head, trying to shake off her foul mood. "You're right. Okay, so I asked Terry if his business was improving since, well, you know, and he got a really funny look on his face."

"Guilt?" Mel asked.

"No," Angie said. "More like caution."

"Hold that thought," Mel said. She hurried to the walk-in and stepped inside. She grabbed two carrot cake cupcakes and kicked the door shut behind her.

"All right, now I'm ready," she said as she sat down and put a cupcake in front of each of them.

"I don't think he suspected that I was fishing," Angie said as she peeled the paper from around her cupcake. "But he was very careful with his answers. He said it was better to have competition, because it raises the bar for the designers to always feel pushed by someone else's work. He also said he was in Los Angeles at a fashion show the night of Christie's death and had loads of witnesses."

"Really? Then what happened?"

"Stupid Tony and Sal came barging in. They told Terry that I had just run away from the convent and was having delusions of getting married. I could have killed them!"

"It was better that you took it out on your phone," Mel said. Her head throbbed where she'd smacked it, and she put her hand up to feel the bump. Sure enough, the goose egg was bigger and sat right in the middle of her cowlick, making her hair stick up. Fabulous.

"What happened to you?"

Mel told her about seeing Alma drive into the garage and the conversation she'd overheard between Terry and Alma.

"It sounds like Terry convinced her to steal the dress Phoebe designed for Christie's wedding, and in return she gets a job there."

"Yeah," Mel agreed. "What I wonder is did they kill her

to get this dress? It seems unlikely, but they both loathed Christie, and certainly neither of them seems sad to see her dead."

"Did you see the gown?" Angie asked.

"Just a glance under the car," Mel said. "Could a gown really incite murder, or is it just the spoils of the tragedy? As in did Alma help herself to the gown because Christie obviously wasn't going to be using it?"

"But if Phoebe's the designer, won't she notice that it's gone missing?" Angie asked.

"They seem to think she's too distraught over Christie's death. It sounds as if she's practically catatonic. Certainly, Terry and Alma weren't worried about her finding out."

The bells jangled on the door, and both Mel and Angie left the kitchen to wait on the customers. Three high school kids from the local prep school—their knee-highs and plaid skirts gave them away—stood jostling one another at the counter.

The girls giggled as they ordered and took their cupcakes to go. The bells jangled again, and several older ladies on a shopping spree, as evidenced by the bags that surrounded them, entered and parked themselves in a booth. More students arrived, as well as a busload of tourists. Not bad for the middle of the afternoon on a weekday.

They spent the next hour in a flurry of cupcakes. It felt good, almost normal, again. When the crush eased and they were loading up trays to restock the front, Angie looked at Mel. Her brown eyes were full of hope, and Mel nodded in understanding.

"We won't lose our business," she said with more confidence than she felt. "Now that we know someone else had a real motive."

"Who had a motive?"

Angie and Mel glanced up; Joe DeLaura was standing

in the doorway. He was wearing a charcoal gray suit with a white dress shirt and a black and burgundy striped tie.

"Hi, Joe," Angie said with a glare that could have melted ice. "Did Tony and Sal send you?"

"Nope, I just came by for a cupcake," he said with a smile. His gaze lingered on Mel's face, making her feel like he was talking about more than her baked goods. She returned his stare, feeling ridiculously breathless.

"Oh, well, what can I get you?" Angie asked, obviously deciding not to enlighten him about her rift with Sal and Tony.

"You pick. I trust your judgment," he said.

Angie glanced between them. "Okay, then, I'll just . . ." Her voice trailed off as she took a full tray to the front of the bakery.

"Hi, Mel," Joe said. He came farther into the kitchen. "How are you?"

"Aside from being falsely suspected of murder and having my business ruined because of it, I'm fine."

"Gonzales and Rayburn are good detectives," he said. "They'll find out who killed Christie Stevens and your name will be cleared."

"I wish I could be so sure," she said. "In the meantime, the media is slapping my reputation around like it's a piñata just because I'm longtime friends with Tate. Even if they catch the real killer, I'm not sure my business will survive the slander."

Angie trotted back into the kitchen with a glass of milk and a Cherry Bomb cupcake. She plopped them down on the table in front of Joe.

"Consider it a bribe," she said. "Just think, if Mel gets arrested, no more cupcakes for you."

He looked stricken, but then gave his sister a dark look. "I can't be bribed."

Angie gave a long-suffering sigh. "Then I'll have to lower myself to threats. Help us, or I'll tell Mom."

"You wouldn't," he said.

"Try me," she returned as she handed him a fork.

"Are you sure you're not a defense attorney?" he asked. "You fight dirty."

"You betcha," Angie said as she headed back to the front.

"Unfortunately, there's not much I can do to help until the investigators arrest someone, and hopefully, it won't be you," he said.

"It might have helped if you hadn't had my uncle Stan taken off the case," Mel complained.

Joe took a bite of the cupcake, and his eyes glazed. "Wow. How do you . . ."

He noticed Mel was frowning at him, and he swallowed with a gulp.

"Sorry. Look, I know it may not seem like it, but I did it to protect both of you. Stan is a lifer with the PD. He can't risk working a case that involves his niece. It would destroy his career. And as for you, what do you think a decent defense attorney would do to you if he found out your uncle was the lead detective?"

Mel refused to acknowledge the little flutter she felt when he said he did it to protect her. She was not that susceptible to his charm—okay, maybe she was, but she didn't have to let him know it.

"I suppose," she said grudgingly.

"Melanie, are you ready to go?"

Mel turned to see Joyce in the doorway. "Hi, Mom. Go where?"

"We have a meeting with the attorney Johnny Dietz recommended. Didn't you get my message?"

"No, it's been crazy here today," Mel said. "Mom, you remember Joe DeLaura, Angie's brother?"

Joyce glanced at Mel and her eyes went wide; even she understood that it didn't look good to be talking about going to a defense attorney in front of an assistant district attorney.

"A lawyer?" Joe asked. He had a mouthful of cupcake, so Mel had to translate what he said, but the implication behind the mumble was obvious. If she was innocent, why did she need an attorney?

"Mom believes in preparing for the worst," Mel said. "She's the only person I know who has an operational bomb shelter in her backyard."

"Hey, if the Palo Verde Nuclear Plant decides to have a big hiccup, I'll be ready," Joyce said. "And what about terrorists? There could be another attack. You never know."

Mel made bug eyes at Joe and he nodded in understanding. Mama DeLaura had been known to show up at her grown children's houses in the middle of the night, just to be sure they were safely tucked into their beds so she could sleep without worrying about them.

"I'd better go," Mel said.

She and Joyce headed towards the door.

"Who's the attorney?" Joe asked. "Maybe I know him."

"Steve Wolfmeier," Joyce said. "Have you heard of him?"

Joe's brows lowered over his eyes like storm clouds on the horizon. "Yeah."

"Care to elaborate?" Mel asked.

"No," Joe said. He stabbed his cupcake with his fork, and Mel had a feeling he was picturing Steve Wolfmeier's head. Interesting.

"Mel, we're going to be late," Joyce said from the doorway. "Don't you want to change into a nice dress?"

Joe glanced up from his cupcake, and his gaze raked Mel

from head to toe, taking in her clingy knit shirt and hip-hugging jeans and all the way down to her suede boots.

"You look fine just the way you are," he said. "In fact, you might want to wear a sweater, preferably a big, bulky shapeless number."

"Well, I don't see how that would help," Joyce said.

Mel felt Joe's gaze on her face, and the intensity of his scrutiny left her feeling flustered. There was history between this Wolfmeier guy and Joe, and she was just the gal to find out what it was.

Fifteen

The firm of Wolfmeier and Jankovich was located in Paradise Valley. It was the richest zip code in the Valley of the Sun, and that alone should have given Mel a clue as to what to expect. Sadly, it did not.

Joyce parked behind a building that looked like a modern nightmare of concrete and glass. They walked past an enormous fountain in the shape of an upside-down pyramid with layers of gray stone forming a shallow pool around it.

The doors to the building were big and thick, and opened into a lobby of ivory marble with deep-rust-colored veins. A secretary wearing an earbud sat at an oversized desk that Joyce approached, clutching her Coach bag with determination.

Mel hung back. She noticed the building had a security desk with an actual guard in uniform stationed by the door. What, exactly, did an attorney need a security guard for, unless he represented some very bad people?

"Come on, Melanie," her mother called from the bank
of elevators beyond the desk. "Mr. Wolfmeier is expecting
us."

The elevator had mirrored walls and plush carpeting,
and a melodic voice announced the floors as they passed.
Mel avoided her reflection, choosing to stare at the carpet
while her mother fixed her lipstick. A bell chimed, and the
elevator stopped on the fifth floor.

Another receptionist greeted them and led them to a
large office that offered a panoramic view of the back of
Camelback Mountain. Mel and Joyce exchanged a look,
and Mel wondered if her eyes looked as nervous as her
mother's.

"Mom," she said, "I don't think we can afford to be
here. In fact, I don't think I can even afford to breathe the
air in here. These guys will probably rob you blind trying
to defend me, when I don't need it."

"Nonsense, they come very highly recommended," said
Joyce. "I can pay whatever it takes."

Mel tipped her head and studied her mom. Since her
father had died, her mother had forged ahead even when
she didn't have a clue, like the time she helped Mel buy her
first car, which was a lemon they got suckered into paying double its value for, but Joyce had not been daunted.
She had parked herself in that auto dealer's showroom and
glowered until she was given a full refund and the clunker
was taken off her hands. It hadn't been easy.

The salesmen had alternately tried charming her and
threatening her, but when Joyce dug in her heels about
something, she generally sprouted roots until she got her
way. It was a quality Mel admired her for; in fact, she admired her mother more than she could ever express.

However, she saw that same root-sprouting expression
on her mother's face now, and that did not bode well for her
or for the attorney. She knew her mother wanted to protect

her, but she didn't want her to lose her life's savings trying to defend Mel for a crime she didn't commit.

It wasn't as if the police had arrested her. Sure, they'd questioned her, confiscated her cupcakes, and searched her bakery, but no charges had been filed; and in her hopeful heart, she hoped none would be.

Mel was about to cup Joyce's elbow and lead her back to the elevator when the door to the office opened and a man in a suit as shiny as sharkskin walked into the room. He was tall and thin; his white hair close cropped in a haircut Mel was sure cost more than her entire outfit. He smiled at them, and his bright blue eyes crinkled in the corners. As he crossed the room, Mel realized he was younger than his hair made him look. She guessed him to be only five years older than herself.

He shook Joyce's hand first. "Mrs. Cooper, I'm Steve Wolfmeier, and this must be your daughter, Melanie."

He turned and shook Melanie's hand. "Nice to meet you."

"You, too, Mr. Wolfmeier."

"Call me Steve." His look should have been smarmy, but somehow he made it charming. Mel felt a reluctant smile curve her lips.

"Have a seat, please," he said. "Can I get you anything?"

"No, we're fine, thank you," Mel said. She didn't want a twenty-dollar latte tacked onto what was sure to be an exorbitant bill.

Joyce looked at her, and Mel shook her head. They sat down in the chairs across from his desk.

"Miss Cooper, may I call you Melanie?" Wolfmeier asked as he sat in the plush seat behind his desk.

"Sure."

"It seems you're a person of interest to the Scottsdale Police," he said.

"So it seems," she agreed.

"What do you have to say about it?" he asked.

"I just found her," Mel said, raising her hands in an "I surrender" gesture. "I had nothing to do with what happened to her."

"You were hired to make the cupcakes for her wedding, correct?"

"Yes."

"And you were delivering those cupcakes when you found her?"

"No, she already had them. Two of her designers picked up the cupcakes the day before. Christie and I were to have a meeting to discuss the samples I sent over."

"All we need is a healthy dose of reasonable doubt. Let's see if we can accomplish that. So, Melanie, the cupcakes were out of your hands for how long?"

"I don't know, let's see . . ." Mel tried to remember. Alma and Phoebe had picked up the cupcakes in the evening, and she was to meet Christie in the morning. "Twelve hours."

"So, you didn't see those cupcakes for twelve hours?" he asked.

"Yes."

"Any idea how many people could have had access to those cupcakes in those twelve hours?"

"No idea," Mel said. She noticed that he kept referring to the twelve hours. "I suppose it would depend upon where Christie kept them and who was around at the time. I know she was doing a photo shoot, but I have no idea how many people were in her studio that night."

Steve Wolfmeier leaned back in his chair and grinned. He looked just like a wolf that had cornered a bunny, and Mel wondered if that was where his ancestors had gotten the name Wolfmeier.

"That will be all, Miss Cooper," he said, as if dismissing her from the witness stand. His eyes lingered on her face, and Mel wondered if he could see the stress and worry seep out of her like a slow leak in an air mattress.

He made it seem so easy and so effortless to cast reasonable doubt. But then, that was probably why he was housed in such a fabulous office. The man was good.

"Mrs. Cooper." Steve Wolfmeier turned to Joyce. "I'm going to have to turn down your case."

"What? Why?" Joyce asked, distraught.

"Your daughter doesn't need me," he said. "I'd be robbing you if I took your money."

Mel wondered if the room was miked. How had he known what she'd said? His gaze met hers, and the blue depths were amused. Oh, yeah, he'd heard her. She felt her face grow warm with embarrassment.

"It's not very polite to listen in on other peoples' conversations," she said.

"It's not polite to believe the worst of a person before you've even met them," he returned.

"Touché," she said. "Does one ill-mannered faux pas cancel out another?"

"It could," he said.

Joyce glanced between them. Mel could tell she was so focused on hiring Steve that she was lost to the conversation.

"What would it take?" she asked.

"I hear you bake a mean cupcake," he said.

"I'll send some over."

"Then all is forgiven."

"So, you'll take the case?" Joyce asked.

"I'll consider a box of cupcakes a retainer," he said. "But I honestly don't think you're going to need my services. From my initial inquiries at the medical examiner's office, although one of the cupcakes was tainted, there was no sign of arsenic in the contents of the victim's stomach. It takes a considerable amount of arsenic to kill, and there were only trace amounts found in the cupcake."

"So you're saying. . . ." Mel hesitated, and he finished for her.

"Someone is trying to frame you, but they're doing a very poor job of it. I don't see you getting arrested even if you are a person of interest."

Mel rose from her seat. She wanted to do a cartwheel, but she resisted the impulse. "Thank you, Mr. Wolfmeier."

Joyce teared up as she pumped his hand in gratitude. If she had been doubtful about Mel's innocence before, now she was fully embracing the fact that Mel was innocent. For that alone, Mel would have baked Mr. Wolfmeier a double order of cupcakes.

Joyce excused herself to use the ladies' room to freshen up, and Mel turned to face Steve. "Can I ask you something?"

"Shoot," he said.

"Do you know Joe DeLaura?" she asked.

His smile hardened until it was brittle. He leaned one hip on the desk and considered her. "We went to law school together."

"Oh." Mel would have liked to ask more questions, but Steve didn't appear forthcoming and she was hesitant to annoy him on the off chance that she might need his services.

He must have picked up on her curiosity, however, because he added, "We were both the top of our class. There was a friendly rivalry between us. Then he went his way and I went mine. Why do you ask?"

"He's my business partner's older brother," she said.

Steve glanced at the notes on top of his desk. "Angela DeLaura is his little sister?"

"Yes. Small world, eh?"

"Don't talk to him," Steve said. His friendly smile and demeanor were wiped away like chalk off a slate.

"Why not?" Mel asked.

"Because he's an assistant DA," Steve said. "He's not a friend or a friend of the family; he's the guy who'll put your cute butt in jail for a very long time if you give him even the tiniest crumb of information that he can twist against you."

"But I'm innocent."

"That doesn't matter," Steve said. He crossed the room to stand in front of her. He was a few inches taller, and she had to crane her neck to meet his eyes. "This is a high-profile case, and the DA has to convict someone. If you say the wrong thing to him, even I, as brilliant as I am, won't be able to save you."

"Is Joe that good of an attorney?" Mel asked.

Steve leaned back and considered her. "He's a terrier. If he decides you're going down, he won't rest until you're locked up and they've thrown away the key."

"I really . . ."

"Don't trust him, don't talk to him, and for God's sake, don't share any information with him," Steve said.

He pressed a card into her hand. "If you need to talk to someone about the case, call me."

He stepped back and seemed to take off his intensity like a man changing a shirt. "I'll be waiting for those cupcakes."

Mel wondered if she'd just dreamt the past few seconds. A horrified part of her was beginning to sift through every conversation she'd had with Joe lately, and weigh how damning it might have been.

She felt a tug on her arm; Joyce had returned from the ladies' room and was ready to go.

"Thanks," she said to Steve, and turned to go.

"Don't forget what I said," he called after her.

Mel could assure him she would not.

Sixteen

Joyce opened her mouth to begin talking as soon as they were in the car. Mercifully, Mel's cell phone began to ring its distinctive *Gone With the Wind* theme music, and she gave her mom an apologetic look.

"Sorry, it's the shop. I have to take this," she said. She flipped the phone open. "Hello."

"You need to get back here immediately," Angie shouted. She sounded panicked, which was disturbing because Angie never panicked.

"What's going on?" Mel asked.

"I can't explain right now. Just hurry."

The line went dead.

"Step on it, Mom," Mel said. "We have a situation."

Joyce looked at her, and Mel rolled her hand towards the window in a gesture that meant "Hurry up."

Ten minutes later, Joyce maneuvered into a spot in front of the shop. Mel was out the door and running before the car came to a stop.

The bells chimed as she yanked the door open. Angie was standing alone in the middle of the store. She looked dazed and bewildered.

Mel grabbed her arms. "Ange, what is it? What's going on?"

"The police brought Tate in for questioning again," she said. Her voice was faint. "Mel, I'm afraid they're going to arrest him."

"Oh, no," Mel moaned.

"What's going on? What happened?" Joyce asked as she hurried through the door.

"The police have taken Tate in for questioning again," Mel said.

"But why?"

"Christie's father is pushing for an arrest," Angie said. "Shelby Grady says he's telling everyone at the country club that Tate did it to get her money."

"But that's ridiculous," Mel said. "Tate is worth way more than she was, which is why she drugged him and faked their engagement."

"Good grief! She drugged him?" Joyce sat down at one of the café tables. "You don't think Tate . . ."

"Absolutely not!" Angie declared with a ferocity that made Joyce blink. "Tate is innocent. He'd never harm anyone. He's the kindest, nicest person I've ever known."

Mel could hear their fifties retro atomic wall clock ticking in the ensuing silence. It seemed so much louder than normal. She looked at the flush that stained Angie's cheeks, and suddenly, she understood.

"You're in love with him," she said.

"Don't be ridiculous!" Angie scoffed. But her voice was without heat. "That's absurd."

Joyce rose from her seat. Her eyes, the eyes that were so like Mel's, were kind as they gazed at Angie. She gave her a one-armed hug around the shoulders and then patted Mel's cheek as she made her way to the door.

"I'm going to leave you girls to sort things out," she said. "Call me if you need me, either of you."

Mel and Angie watched her go. Mel mouthed "I love you, Mom," and her mother nodded before she shut the door behind her.

"Why didn't you tell me?"

"There's nothing to tell."

"Don't," Mel said. She felt oddly betrayed and hurt that Angie had feelings for Tate and she'd never said a word. "Don't make it worse."

Angie looked at her, and her large brown eyes looked sad.

"When did it happen?" Mel asked.

"The day you introduced him to me in sixth grade," Angie said.

"Twenty-two years ago?" Mel asked. She sat down in her mother's abandoned chair. "You know, you might have mentioned it somewhere along the line."

"You sound mad."

"I am mad," Mel confirmed. "You're supposed to be my best friend. You're supposed to tell me when you fall in love with someone, no matter who that someone is."

"Oh, like you're so forthcoming with your feelings," Angie chided her.

"What's that supposed to mean?"

"I've seen the way you look at Joe," Angie said. "Don't tell me you see him only as your best friend's brother."

"That's different."

"Different how?" Angie leaned over the table, getting into Mel's space. "You can't have it both ways. You can't expect full disclosure from me and hold your own stuff back."

"What I feel for Joe is just a stupid crush left over from

middle school," Mel argued. "That's not how you feel about Tate. You're in love with him, and I can't believe you never told me."

"How could I," Angie asked, "when he's always been in love with you?"

Mel felt as if Angie had just kicked the chair out from under her.

"No, he hasn't."

"Yes, he has," Angie contradicted her. Her enormous brown eyes were so full of pain that they looked bruised. "He told me so."

"When?" Mel asked.

"Do you remember when we came to visit you while you were studying in Paris?"

"Yes."

"You know we flew over on his company's corporate jet?"

Mel nodded. She didn't want to hear this—no, she didn't. She hated seeing how devastated Angie looked when recounting the story. She glanced down at her hands and realized she'd just shredded a paper napkin that she didn't even remember taking out of the holder.

"Well, we had too much champagne, and I got silly." Bright red splotches lit up Angie's cheekbones, and Mel knew she was horribly embarrassed. Angie swallowed, and continued. "I sort of threw myself at Tate, and we . . . uh . . . well, we joined the mile high club, as it were."

"Oh, no!"

"Oh, yes," Angie replied. "Afterwards, we both agreed it had been a huge mistake. He made me promise we'd never tell you because, and I quote, 'I love her and couldn't bear to lose her.' "

"No," Mel said. Her throat was tight, and she felt as if something she held precious was shattering into a million pieces and she wasn't going to be able to fix it.

"Yes," Angie said. Her mouth lifted at the corners. "All these years your mom has been pushing you and Tate together, and if you'd just given him the nod, he'd be married to you now."

Mel put her head down on the table, feeling slightly sick.

"Why didn't you tell me this?" she asked.

"Let's see." Angie ticked off the reasons on her fingers. "I was mortified. I was crushed. And somehow, 'I've seen Tate naked' isn't as easy to work into a conversation as you might think."

Mel raised her head and gave her a weak smile.

"Look, you two are my best friends. I couldn't risk losing either of you," Angie said.

"But if you told . . ."

"You know what?" Angie interrupted. "I really don't want to talk about this anymore."

"But . . ."

"No," Angie said with a shake of her head. "I'm going to call Joe and see if he can tell me anything about what's happening to Tate."

"If you . . ."

"I'm not going to change my mind," Angie interrupted again. "And I want you to promise that you'll never tell Tate how I feel."

Mel looked at her friend. Her face could have been set in concrete. Mel knew there was no negotiating.

"Pinky swear," Angie said.

Mel felt her lips curve. She linked her right pinky with Angie's. Then she crossed her fingers behind her back.

"No crosses count," Angie said, and Mel let out an exasperated huff. "Swear."

"I swear I won't tell Tate," she said.

"Thank you." Angie unlocked her little finger from Mel's. "Can you man the shop while I go call Joe?"

Mel nodded. There was no one in the shop. Even for midafternoon, it was remarkably dead. She wondered if the rumor that she was a murderer was driving business away. Then she wondered who would believe it. And her thoughts turned back to Joe. Was Steve Wolfmeier right about him? Would Joe get her in his sights as a murderer and be a terrier with her?

She felt a flutter of unease. She had thought that by now, things would be better, that the police would have a suspect in custody who wasn't herself or Tate. Instead, she had more questions than answers, and every time she turned around there was new information that was horrifying, disturbing, or just plain shocking. Angie in love with Tate—why hadn't she seen that one coming?

Mel felt a pang of guilt. She knew she hadn't seen it because she hadn't wanted to. When she thought back on it now, it all made sense. Angie seldom dated, and when she did, it was reluctantly, and she never went out on their movie night. Also, her intense dislike of Christie made more sense now than ever. Mel had thought Angie just didn't like her, but no, it must have been eating her alive that Tate was going to get married.

A hideous thought wiggled into Mel's brain like a worm into a rotten apple. Could Angie have . . . No!

She shook her head. She was not going there. No matter how Angie felt about Tate getting married, if it was what he wanted, she'd never do anything to jeopardize his happiness. And even with her firecracker temper, Angie had never caused anyone real harm. Well, except for the broken nose she had given Jeff Stanton when he called Mel a fatso one time too many.

Mel stood up from the table and started pacing. Whether she liked it or not, it seemed the police liked her or Tate for the crime. The only solution was to find the real killer. Both Terry and Alma looked good for it, but she needed more proof than a stolen wedding gown.

She needed to talk to someone in Christie's inner circle. She wasn't going to get anything more out of Alma. She needed to talk to someone else. She needed to talk to Phoebe.

She hated intruding upon the girl's grief, but enough was enough. She needed to know who wanted Christie dead, and Phoebe was her best untapped source.

"He's been released," Angie said as she stepped back into the room. "He's going home to decompress to some old Clint Eastwood spaghetti Westerns. We should go over after we close and check on him."

" 'I've never seen so many men wasted so bad,' " Mel quoted.

"We'll see," Angie said. "I don't know if it's a *The Good, The Bad and The Ugly* night or a *Two Mules for Sister Sara* night."

"I'd go with Shirley MacLaine, but he may be anti-women right now," Mel said.

"Luckily, I don't count." Angie's voice was wry, and Mel felt bad for her. They still needed to talk about the situation, but Mel would let it rest for now.

"Is it just me, or do we seem abnormally dead?" Mel asked. "I mean, I know the newspaper article may have turned our locals against us, but surely the tourists don't know."

"You're right," Angie said. "I should have sold at least three hundred cupcakes by now, but I'm guessing I've only sold a couple dozen."

"This murder has to be solved quickly," Mel said.

"Before we lose everything."

The phone behind the counter rang, and Mel hurried to answer it.

"Good afternoon, Fairy Tale Cupcakes, how may I help you?"

"Hello, bride killer," the caller said.

Mel sucked in a breath. It was Solomon Singh, owner of the posh jewelry store around the corner.

"I didn't kill her."

"Sure you didn't." Solomon was from India and his accent was faint, as if faded from years of living in the States, but he retained just enough of it to sound exotic and condescending.

"Is there something I can do for you, Solomon?" she asked.

"Yes, you can tell whoever is plastering the streets with these notices of you being wanted for murder to stop putting them on my windows. They clash with my diamond displays."

"Excuse me? What notices?"

"Don't tell me they haven't tagged you?" he asked. He sounded annoyed. "I'd have thought your place would have been covered in them. Look outside for an obnoxious yellow paper."

Mel dropped the phone and raced towards the door.

"What is it?" Angie asked, following her. Mel glanced up and down the street. She felt her vision swim as she saw literally hundreds of yellow notices plastering all available surfaces.

She snatched one off the wall of the western wear store next door. As her eyes skimmed over the page, she felt her hands begin to shake.

In the center there was a picture of her holding a tray of cupcakes with the shop's logo above her. Below the picture was printed: *Community Advisory: Melanie Cooper is a suspect in the murder of Christie Stevens. Anyone with any information is encouraged to call the Scottsdale Police Department.*

"You've got to be kidding me!" Angie blustered from behind her. "That's a total lie! Who would do . . . ?"

Their gazes met, and they both said, "Olivia Puckett."

Mel wadded up the paper and stuffed it in the nearest trash can.

"I'm going to track her down and rip her hair out by the roots!" Angie spat.

"C'mon," Mel said. She would have liked nothing more than to steam over to Olivia's shop and blast her, but they needed to do damage control first. She fished a key out of her pocket and locked up the shop. "Let's gather all of these first."

They worked opposite sides of the street, ripping down the sheets that had been attached to every single telephone pole, bench, and storefront they passed. The sheer boldness of the maneuver took Mel's breath away. When she got to the tattoo parlor on the corner, Mick, one of the tattoo artists, stepped outside, away from the busy buzz of the needles at work inking skin behind him, and handed Mel a stack of yellow papers.

Mick was six foot four, with large gauges in his earlobes that created dime sized holes, a shaved head that sported a rising Phoenix tattoo, and sleeves of brilliantly colorful tattoos running up and down his arms and legs. Oh, and he had several implants in his forehead that looked like horns about to sprout. In short, he looked terrifying, but Mel had discovered over the past few months that he was really a big sweetie who kept an eye out for the neighborhood, loved coconut cupcakes, and had season tickets to the Arizona Opera. The guy had layers.

"These were all over my shop and the ones around the corner. Pretty nasty publicity," he said. "Who did you piss off?"

"Rival baker," Mel said.

"In the 'hood?" he asked.

"No, she's on the other side of 40th Street, in Arcadia," Mel said.

"Well, she's certainly got it in for you. If it's any consolation, I've talked to the others and no one believes it, except Solomon, but he always thinks the worst of everyone."

The sympathy in his voice made Mel want to cry. She swallowed past the lump in her throat, and said, "Thanks, Mick."

"Do you want me to go have a talk with her?" he asked. His blue eyes lit up at the prospect.

Mel was pretty sure Mick would give Olivia a flat-out heart attack, so it was a very tempting offer.

"Thanks, but I think I'd better deal with her on my own."

Mick patted her shoulder with a large hand. "Tell me if you change your mind."

"I will," she promised.

It took the better part of an hour to canvass Old Town and gather all of the libelous papers. By the time she was done, Mel was so angry, she was afraid she might do Olivia an injury.

"I think we got them all," Angie said as she dumped them into the recycle bin in the office.

"Let's keep a couple in case we need proof of harassment," Mel said. "Although I'm quite sure she made certain she left no fingerprints on them."

"You know, I thought she was nuts with the drive-bys and all, but now I think she's certifiable. The woman should be locked up."

"Don't tell Tate about this," Mel said. "He's got enough on his plate."

"Aren't you going to come with me to see him?" Angie asked.

"I don't think that's a good idea. There's too much speculation about us as it is. I don't want to cause him any more problems."

Angie studied her for a moment. "You promise this isn't about what I told you? I couldn't stand it if I messed all of us up because I'm an idiot."

"You're not an idiot," Mel said, and she looped an arm around her friend's shoulders. "You can't help how you feel."

"Believe me, I've tried," Angie said. "I don't want to feel this way, and I wish I didn't."

"We don't choose who we love," Mel said comfortingly.

"So if you're not coming with me, what are you going to do?"

"I'm going to have a little chat with Olivia."

"Oh, I'm totally coming with you," Angie said. She looked like she was ready to rumble.

"No, you're not. This is between me and her."

"But . . ." Angie began to protest, but Mel interrupted. "No, Tate needs you, and besides, you know you have a temper. I haven't always been patient with her. But despite my frosting her windshield, I still think I'll be able to stay calm when I deal with Olivia."

"What're you saying?"

"That you have a tendency to lead with your fists, and I don't want that kind of trouble."

"I haven't hit anyone in ages," Angie protested.

"You popped a guy with an uppercut when he patted your butt at the Salty Senorita last week," Mel reminded her.

"I was teaching him some manners," Angie protested.

Mel smiled. "No doubt he won't do that again, but I can't have anything like that go down with Olivia. You're not going. End of discussion."

"Call me as soon as you talk to her," Angie said.

"I promise."

"And you'd better make her cry, or I'll be disappointed."

"I'll do my best," Mel said.

They closed the shop and parted with a hug.

Mel climbed into her Mini Cooper and shot across Old Town Scottsdale. She turned south on 68th Street and then headed west on Indian School Road.

She reached 40th Street and turned into the parking lot of a small strip mall. Confections Bakery sat between a trophy maker and a florist. A quick glance told Mel that, unlike her bakery, Confections was busy. Several cars were parked in front, and she could see a line of customers milling about in front of the display cases. She felt her temper heat again, and she forced herself to breathe slowly in and out.

Mel took one of the papers she had collected and strode across the parking lot. She was going to be calm but firm. Olivia Puckett's obsession with her shop had to stop right now. She had enough to contend with, without dealing with her crazy smear campaign.

If it came right down to it, Mel was not afraid to call in the law. Given her current relationship with the Scottsdale Police, she figured Steve Wolfmeier might have to be her front, but she suspected he'd be okay with that. He looked like the type who could throw out enough legal jargon to choke a donkey, and Olivia certainly qualified as that.

Mel pulled open the door to the bakery and approached the counter. Several hair-netted women stood behind it, wearing white polyester smocks with their names embroidered in black on the left breast. Mel approached a large woman who looked to be in charge of the counter because she was barking orders at the others.

"Excuse me," she said. "I'm looking for Olivia Puckett."

"Take a number," the woman barked.

"Pardon?"

The woman waved a beefy arm towards a red plastic ticket dispenser. "Take a number."

"I just want to talk . . ." Mel began, but the woman glared at her and pointed to the ticket machine again.

"I'll just take a number," Mel said.

The woman nodded and yelled, "Seventy-six."

Mel glanced at the pink ticket in her hand. She was eighty-three. Terrific.

She waited through an order of cookies, three pies, two birthday cakes, and two more orders of cookies, before the stout woman finally called, "Eighty-three."

Mel approached the counter. "I would like to speak with Olivia Puckett, please."

"You don't want to buy anything?" the woman asked. Her nose was large and hooked, and her eyes were bulbous like a toad's.

"No, as I tried to tell you before, I'm here to see Olivia," Mel said. She knew her voice sounded snippy, but so far the only good thing that had come of this visit was the fact that no one in front of her had bought any cupcakes. It was small satisfaction, but she'd take it.

"Olivia's not here," the woman said.

Mel glanced at the name embroidered on her chest. "Well, June, do you know when she'll be back?"

"She won't," June said. "She's off to see her mother in that assisted-care facility on Thomas Road, Serenity Springs. Her mother is senile, you know, crazy as a bedbug."

Perhaps that explained Olivia's behavior, Mel thought. Maybe the whole Puckett family tree was forked. She glanced at her watch. She'd waited twenty minutes for nothing. Well, it was not going to be for nothing. She was going to hunt Olivia down at Serenity Springs and have it out with her once and for all.

"Thanks," she said and helped herself to one of the sample cookies on the counter. She took a bite, and at the door, she spun around. "Try using some lemon zest in these sugar cookies. It makes all the difference."

June shrugged at her as if she couldn't care less what the

cookies tasted like. Well, if nothing else, Mel now knew her help was far superior to Olivia's. Even on her most surly day, Angie was a gracious hostess.

She climbed back into her car and headed south to Thomas Road. Serenity Springs was a posh assisted-care facility, and Mel knew Olivia's bakery must be doing quite well if she could afford this sort of care for her mother.

She pulled in and scanned the lot until she saw Olivia's pink nightmare of a van parked near the entrance. Bingo!

She took the flyer and strode towards the building. Again, she coached herself on her behavior. She wasn't going to cause a scene. She was just going to be very firm, letting Olivia know that she had better back off or there would be severe consequences. She was going to use calm, cool reasoning. If that didn't work, she'd just have to go to plan B. Too bad she didn't really have a plan B.

Seventeen

Two sets of sliding doors opened when Mel stepped on the large black mat. She strode into the lobby, which was decorated in dark woods and beige marble but didn't seem oppressive because there were floor-to-ceiling windows all around that let in the daylight.

A pretty young woman in a bright red suit was working at the reception desk. Her name tag read Grace. Mel approached the desk with her most winning smile.

"Hi, I'm here to see Olivia Puckett," she said.

Grace frowned in thought. "I don't know a resident by that name. We have an Anna Puckett in room 363. Isn't Olivia her daughter?"

"Yes, she is," Mel said. "She's expecting me. We're meeting here to discuss some business."

"I'll ring to let them know to expect you," Grace said. "And your name?"

Mel blanked. She didn't want to give Olivia a heads-up. She'd freak out if she knew Mel was here. She'd probably call the police, and that was the last thing Mel needed.

"Your name, ma'am?"

"Sarah McAllister," Mel said, surprised by her own lie. It was the name of the food critic for the local paper, and a pretty brilliant fib. "I'm here to interview her for the paper."

"Oh, I love your column, Ms. McAllister. I read it every Wednesday." The woman smiled and handed her a clip-on visitor's badge. She dialed a house phone, waited a bit, and then hung up. "There's no answer, but since she's expecting you, I'll just send you on down. Now, you want to head straight down the hall and turn to the right; Mrs. Puckett's room is halfway down on your left."

"Thank you," Mel said.

She strode away from the desk. She felt a little bad about lying, but she needed to clear the air with Olivia once and for all. She suspected Olivia was with her mother today in an attempt to avoid this confrontation, which she had to know was coming. Well, Mel couldn't let her get away with it. It was one thing to stalk her shop, but it was another to slander her in her own neighborhood.

She turned right as directed and glanced up ahead. In what appeared to be a small lounge area, she saw a woman standing in front of the tall windows beside an elderly lady in a wheelchair. The giveaway was the wiry gray topknot on her head. As she bent over the woman in the chair, Olivia's broad features held an unexpected softness, a compassion Mel would not have expected of her.

She watched as Olivia smoothed her mother's white hair back from her face.

"Look, Mama," Olivia said as she pointed out the window, "there are those lovebirds we saw last week. I think they came back to say hi to you."

The elderly woman made a small grunting sound, as if she had lost her power of speech.

Olivia tenderly tucked a light blanket around her mother's legs and a shawl around her frail shoulders.

"Do you suppose they were somebody's pets and now they're free?" Olivia asked. Her voice sounded wistful.

Mel stepped back into the shadows. She felt like a heel. No matter what Olivia had done to her, she had no right to intrude upon her time with her mother. Their discussion could wait for another time.

She turned and was headed toward the door when she heard Olivia's shrill voice.

"What are *you* doing here?"

Mel glanced over her shoulder, fearful that Olivia was talking to her. But no, she was chastising someone wearing scrubs. From the back, it appeared to be a man in his early twenties.

"I thought they fired you!" Olivia snapped. Any compassion she had shown her mother vanished as she lashed out at the unfortunate worker. "I know you've been taking her fentanyl. I've been counting every day, and some are always missing. What are you doing, selling it?"

There was a muttered reply that Mel couldn't hear.

"Don't lie to me!" Olivia snapped. She grabbed the handles of her mother's chair and began pushing her in Mel's direction. "I'll have you fired yet!"

This was definitely not the best time to talk to Olivia. Mel beat a hasty retreat towards the lobby.

"Ms. McAllister," Grace called as she approached. "Did you find Ms. Puckett? I tried ringing her room again, but no one answered."

"It's fine," Mel said, removing her visitor's badge. "She seems busy. Perhaps another time."

The young woman's face got tight. "Not again."

"I'm sorry?" Mel asked.

"Someone has been stealing Mrs. Puckett's pain patches, and her daughter thinks it's someone on staff, but it isn't."

By her fiercely protective tone, Mel guessed there was something between the young receptionist and the man

Olivia had been accusing. Mel was doubly glad that she hadn't stormed in on Olivia. She certainly didn't want to be stepping into the midst of a drama.

"Well, I'll just be on my way," Mel said.

"Should I tell Miss Puckett you stopped by?" Grace asked.

"Oh, no," Mel said. "I wouldn't want her to feel awkward. I'll just pop into her shop tomorrow."

"That's probably for the best," Grace agreed.

Mel stepped back through the automatic doors and crossed the parking lot to her car. She rounded a minivan and smacked into a slender blonde who looked as if she'd been crying.

"Phoebe?" Mel asked, stunned to have run into the young designer.

Phoebe blinked at her through teary eyes, and Mel watched her struggle to gain her composure.

"Are you all right?" Mel asked.

"No," Phoebe snapped. "My grampy's dying. I'm very far from all right."

"I'm so sorry," Mel said.

"Why are you here?" Phoebe asked, her tone ripe with hostility.

"Visiting someone," Mel said. It wasn't a total lie, and maybe it would get her a sympathy vote.

Phoebe fished through her silver bag until she found a small packet of tissues. She wiped her eyes and blew her nose.

"Well, if you'll excuse me . . ."

"Actually, I'd like to ask you some questions," Mel said.

"Why would I talk to you?" Phoebe asked. Her eyes were hard. Her upper lip curled in a sneer. "I heard they think her fiancé, your friend, murdered Christie."

"He didn't," Mel said. It came out more defensive

than she would have liked, and Phoebe looked even more suspicious.

"I'm trying to find out who did kill Christie before an innocent person is wrongly convicted."

Phoebe tossed her long blonde hair over her shoulder with a humph. She obviously didn't believe Mel.

"I thought you baked cupcakes for a living," Phoebe said. "I had no idea you were an investigator, too. Do detectives Gonzales and Rayburn know you're on the case?"

Mel got the feeling that Phoebe was trying to provoke her. The young woman had her head tilted to the side and was watching her like a cat scrutinizing a fish in a fishbowl.

"You were close to Christie, weren't you?" Mel asked.

"More than close," Phoebe said. She glanced over her shoulder at the building and then began to walk towards her car. She didn't invite her, but Mel walked beside her anyway.

"Did Christie confide to you that she was afraid of someone?"

"Afraid? She wasn't afraid of anyone. People adored her," Phoebe said. "She was a visionary."

"Then why was she trying to trap Tate Harper into marrying her?" Mel asked.

Phoebe glared. "She wasn't. She didn't."

"She drugged him and then convinced him that he proposed to her when he didn't," Mel said.

"I don't know anything about that," Phoebe said.

"Really?" Mel asked. Then she decided to bluff. "Alma says you helped her."

"I did not," Phoebe protested, but she glanced away, not meeting Mel's eyes. "Alma's just jealous. She always was."

"Jealous of what?"

"My relationship with Christie. She knew I was more

talented than Alma, so she invested more time in me. We were gal pals. We went shopping together and got manicures, we even dieted together, which Alma would never do."

"So you were friends," Mel said.

"More like sisters," Phoebe said. Her voice broke, and she looked as if she was about to cry again.

"I'm sorry," Mel said.

"Yeah, I'm sure you are," Phoebe sniffed. Her voice was thick with sarcasm, and Mel sighed.

"Look, this is none of my business," Mel said. "But maybe you should know."

"What?" Phoebe paused with her car door open.

"Terry Longmore has hired Alma to work in his studio."

"So?" Phoebe asked. "They were both jealous of me and Christie; they deserve each other."

"Maybe, but Terry hired Alma on the condition that she deliver Christie's wedding gown to him," Mel said. "As I understand it, Alma took it from the studio and turned it over to Terry for the promise of a design job."

Phoebe stared at her for a moment, as if she couldn't believe what Mel as saying. Then she shrugged.

"Given that Christie's dead, I don't suppose it really matters now, does it?"

"But it's your design," Mel said.

Phoebe tipped her head toward the building behind them. "I have bigger things to worry about."

Mel watched her climb into her sports car and drive away. She sensed Phoebe was trying to put some distance between them, which wasn't a complete surprise if she thought that Mel had murdered her beloved mentor.

She drove back to her apartment in Old Town feeling as if she had accomplished nothing. The sun had slipped below the horizon and the orange sky was being brushed like an artist's canvas with the broad lilac strokes of the coming twilight.

Mel wondered how Tate was doing, and which movie he and Angie were watching. Then she thought about Angie's feelings for Tate, and selfishly wished she didn't know. She didn't want their dynamic to get messed up because Angie liked Tate more than she should. Mel rejected Angie's idea that Tate felt more for her than friendship. She figured that, being a man, that had probably been the first excuse he could come up with to let Angie down easily. But then, why didn't he like Angie?

She was beautiful and funny and smart, a fiercely loyal friend, certainly a better catch than Christie Stevens. What had he been thinking to get involved with that? And now that she thought of it, this whole thing was Tate's fault for getting involved with that egomaniac in the first place.

Deep in her brooding, Mel didn't notice the person waiting in the shadows of her apartment stairs until it was too late. He shoved off the wall and stepped towards her. She leapt back with a gasp.

A hand reached out to grab her, and Mel didn't hesitate. Using her purse, she smacked her would-be assailant in the head with all her might.

"Ouch!" a male voice grunted. Mel turned to run for help, but then he said, "Mel, it's Joe."

"Joe? Delaura?" she asked stupidly. "What are you doing lurking in the dark? What if I had a gun?"

"I shudder to think," he said dryly. "What do you have in that purse, rocks?"

He had a hand pressed to his temple, and Mel saw a thin trickle of blood run down the side of his face.

"Oh, no, you're hurt," she said. Her voice was shaky from the rush of adrenaline, and she put her hand over her chest as if she could calm her racing heart. "Let's get you into the kitchen and wash that cut."

He pulled his fingers away. "It's just a scrape."

"Scrapes don't trickle," she said. She unlocked the door and flipped on the light. "Go."

"You closed early tonight." He sounded disappointed.

Mel felt a small smile tip her lips. "Don't tell me you're here for cupcakes. The shop is closed, maybe for good."

She tried to keep the self-pitying tone out of her voice, really she did, and failed miserably.

"Angie told me about the posters," he said. "Are you sure it was Olivia Puckett?"

She gave him a look and led him over to the sink. She ran the water until it was warm and then put a paper towel under it. The cut on his forehead really was more of a scrape. Nevertheless, she pressed the wet towel against it and held it there.

She glared at him. Steve Wolfmeier's warning echoed in her ears, and she didn't want to discuss anything with Joe that might land her in an unflattering black-and-white striped pantsuit.

"What?" he asked. He plunked his hands on his hips and smiled at her. It was a Joe DeLaura special, all dimples and white teeth, that made her brain fog up like steam on a windowpane.

"I'm not supposed to talk to you about anything," she said. "Not even the weather."

"Says who?" he asked.

"Steve Wolfmeier."

"He's your attorney?"

"Sort of," she said. "He wouldn't take the case, but he did say that I shouldn't talk to you, that you're a terrier, and if you decide I'm guilty, then I'm as good as locked up."

Joe frowned and leaned close. His face was just inches from hers when he said, "I don't know if I should be flattered or offended."

"It didn't sound like praise."

"What did it sound like?"

He was standing inside the edge of her personal space. Mel tried to be okay with it, but his presence was a bit overwhelming, as if he inhaled more than his share of the oxygen between them.

"It sounded like you two have a history," she said. "And not a nice one."

Joe raised his eyebrows in surprise and stepped back. Mel lowered her arms and examined the towel. It had a smudge of blood from the cut, but a glance at his temple revealed that the bleeding had stopped. She felt the air whoosh out of her lungs, which surprised her; she hadn't realized she was holding her breath. Assaulting an assistant DA would do that for you, she supposed.

"You're very astute," he said. "We were friends in law school, but it ended badly."

"Grades or a girl?"

"A little bit of both."

An awkward silence in which Mel desperately wanted to grill him about his past, which good manners forbade, ensued. She resisted. Barely.

"Are you hungry?" she asked. "I'm sure to have cupcakes that need to be eaten. Not the healthiest choice for dinner, but I think I can live with it."

"I thought the shop was closed," he said. "And that you weren't to talk to me."

"I changed my mind," she said. "Steve Wolfmeier is not the boss of me. Besides, someone needs to help get rid of my inventory. Coffee?"

"That'd be great," he answered as he prowled around the kitchen.

Mel fussed with the coffeepot, thinking that if someone had told her when she was twelve that Joe DeLaura would be standing in her cupcake bakery awaiting coffee and cupcakes with her, she'd have keeled over on the spot.

"Can you grab some plates and forks?" She gestured towards the cupboard over the triple-basin sink.

"Sure," he said.

Mel let the coffee drip and headed into the walk-in with a tray. She pulled four of her favorites and headed back out to the kitchen.

She filled two mugs with hot coffee and added them to the tray. Joe was already sitting when she joined him at the worktable. She put a mug in front of him while he debated which of the cupcakes on the tray he wanted.

"Why cupcakes?" he asked.

She knew he was asking why she made only cupcakes and nothing else.

"They're happy," she answered. "I like to think they remind people of the simple pleasures of childhood. Well, that and it's a lot easier to justify buying yourself a cupcake than it is a whole cake, so it seemed like good economics, too."

"My mom used to bake cupcakes for our birthday parties," Joe said. "I always asked for vanilla with chocolate icing."

"I wonder what that says about you," Mel said. She reached onto the tray, found a vanilla cupcake with chocolate icing, and put it on his plate.

"Let me guess," he said. "That I'm as bland as day-old bread."

"Or you enjoy the subtleties in life found in the compatibly married flavors of vanilla and chocolate."

Joe laughed out loud. "Nice spin. I forgot you were once a marketing whiz kid. You're good, very good."

Mel smiled. "Maybe I should make up personality matches for cupcakes. It might be the only thing that saves the shop."

"Business has slowed?" he asked.

Mel watched as he took a bite of his cupcake. She felt a

surge of satisfaction when his eyes glazed over just a little bit.

"Yeah, thanks to Olivia getting the word out that I'm a murder suspect," she said.

She took a Red Velvet cupcake off the tray and peeled off the paper. She stuck her fork into the cream cheese frosting, appreciating how the fork glided smoothly into the cake below. She mouthed the cake off of the fork, and when she glanced up, Joe was watching her with an intensity that made her throat go dry. To keep from choking, she took a quick swallow of coffee.

They finished their cupcakes in silence, but Mel was aware of every gesture Joe made, the way he blew on his coffee before he sipped, and the way he licked the corners of his mouth after a bite of cupcake. It was excruciating.

"So, what brought you here tonight?" she asked, pushing her plate away.

"I don't know," he said. His brown eyes were steady when they met hers. "Honestly, it's career suicide for me to be here, fraternizing with a suspect."

"But you can't resist my cupcakes," she teased, trying to lessen the tension between them.

He looked at her and said, "Something like that."

"Something?" she asked.

"You need to steer clear of Steve Wolfmeier," he said. "He's bad news."

"And so we've come full circle in our conversation," Mel said. "I appreciate that you two have a history, but I need protection."

"Why?" he asked.

"You're kidding, right?"

His face was set. Not kidding.

"Ever since I found the body, I've been targeted by the police and the media as the most likely suspect just because Tate and I are friends. And now Olivia Puckett is using it to try and run me out of business. What am I supposed to do? I need help."

"Find someone else," he said.

"How is this any of your business?" she asked.

"You're my sister's business partner," he said. "I'm looking out for her interests."

That stung, although Mel wasn't sure why. Maybe because a part of her had hoped he was looking out for her.

"Well, don't worry your pretty little head about Angie, she'll be fine," Mel said. She glanced pointedly at the clock. "Shouldn't you be shuffling along to attend to your little colleague? She must be wondering where you are by now."

"How is that relevant?" Joe asked. He rose from the table, gathering their plates and mugs, and headed to the sink. He began to wash the dishes, but Mel stomped over and shut off the water.

"Don't bother," she said. "I'll take care of it myself."

"Why are you so angry?" he asked, spinning to face her.

"Do you think I'm guilty?" she asked. There—she'd said it. She watched him watching her. He didn't answer right away.

She spun away from him and strode to the back door. She pushed it open and gestured for him to go.

"Good night, Joe."

"Mel, I don't think . . ." he began, but she interrupted, "Too little, too late. Good night."

He strode past her and out the door. His jaw was clenched, and he looked as irritated as she felt.

"Mel," he said. She glanced up at him, and his brown eyes were narrowed in concern. "Be careful."

She said nothing, not trusting her voice, and shut the door with a definitive click.

Eighteen

Mel used an ice cream scoop to fill the paper-lined compartments of the cupcake pan with batter. The scoop was the perfect tool to keep the cupcakes uniform in size. She was making a big batch, using her thirty-five-cupcake tin.

This batch was called Moonlight Madness, because these were the cupcakes she always made in the middle of the night when she couldn't sleep, like tonight. It was a simple chocolate cupcake with vanilla buttercream frosting rolled in coconut and a Hershey Kiss planted in the middle of the frosting. Mostly, she made these because she could eat all the Hershey Kisses she wanted while baking. Tonight, however, even a fistful of kisses wasn't lifting her mood.

Mel opened the door to her industrial-sized convection oven and slid the large tin onto the middle rack. She set her cupcake-shaped timer for twenty minutes and began to clean the steel worktable.

The strains of the theme from *Gone With the Wind* interrupted the quiet, and Mel grabbed her cell phone off the counter. Who would be calling her at one o'clock in the morning?

She checked the number. It was Tate.

"What are you doing up so late?" she asked.

" 'When you have insomnia, you're never really asleep, and you're never really awake,' " he said.

"The best you can do is a quote from *Fight Club*?" she asked. "Hardly a classic, you must have insomnia."

"It's a classic guy flick, I don't expect you to appreciate it," he returned.

"Huh," she grunted. "How did you know I was awake?"

"Because Angie and I are standing outside the back door," he said.

Mel whirled around, and sure enough, she could see their outlines backlit against the window shade.

She hurried across the kitchen to unbolt the door. "Why didn't you use your keys?"

"We didn't want to scare you," Tate said.

They grinned at each other as she swung the door wide.

"I think you two can hang up now," Angie said as she strode around Tate. "Oh, kisses! Is it a Moonlight Madness night?"

"Technically, I think there's a new moon out tonight, but yeah, I couldn't sleep."

"We figured," Angie said. "We just finished watching the last spaghetti Western and thought we'd check on you. How did it go with Olivia? Did you make her cry?"

They pulled up stools around the worktable, and Mel passed out Hershey Kisses like she was dealing cards.

"No. In fact, I never spoke to her," she said.

"What?" Angie demanded.

Mel told them the whole story from start to finish.

About Olivia's frail-looking mother and how compassion-ate Olivia was while taking care of her.

"Now why'd you go and tell me that?" Angie grumped. "I don't want to feel sorry for that woman."

"Me either," Mel admitted. "But I can't help it."

"What if she pulls another stunt like the last?" Tate asked. "You can't let her mess with your business."

"I know," Mel said. "Maybe I'll just have to appeal to her gentler side."

Angie and Tate gave her matching dubious looks, and she shrugged.

"It really isn't going to matter what Olivia does to me if the police don't find Christie's killer soon," Mel said. "The bad press will do us in more swiftly than any of her shenanigans."

"Let's revisit our suspects," Tate suggested. "There's me."

"No," Angie and Mel said together.

"There's you." He pointed at Mel with a Hershey Kiss.

"No," they chorused again.

"There's Terry Longmore," he said. "And now that we know he's signed on Alma and had her steal a gown for his studio, there's motive."

"But he has an alibi," Angie argued. "He was at a fash-ion show in Los Angeles."

"Has that been verified?" Tate asked.

Mel peeled off the tiny strip of foil stuck on her kiss. "The police must have checked it out."

"We should find out for sure," Tate said.

"I'll call Uncle Stan," Mel said.

"What about that weird Alma girl?" Angie asked. "I got a very bad feeling about her from the start."

"She said she had an alibi," Mel said. "Although she never said what it was."

"We need to find out what it is," Tate said.

"I'll pay her a visit tomorrow," Mel promised. "That way she can't duck me. Maybe if I let her know that I know she took the gown, I can use it as leverage to force her to tell me what she knows."

Angie frowned. "Be careful. If she's a murderer, she won't hesitate to hurt you in order to protect herself."

"I don't think you should go alone," Tate added. "It could be dangerous."

"I don't think she'll talk to me if anyone is with me," Mel countered.

The timer rang, and Mel hopped off her stool to get the cakes out of the oven. She tested the top of one by gently pressing it with her fingertip. When it sprang back, she knew they were done.

She placed the large tin on a wire rack to cool and started to gather her ingredients for the frosting. She had used her industrial Hobart mixer for the batter, so she decided to go with her pink KitchenAid for the frosting. The butter had softened nicely, and she let the mixer cream it while she took a large bottle of clear vanilla extract out of the pantry. She liked to use clear because it kept the frosting a bright white or, in this case, a glowing moon color. Angie added the sugar cup by cup, and then Tate assisted by adding the milk until the frosting was the perfect consistency.

Mel marveled at how the three of them worked silently together, never getting in one another's way. She supposed twenty-two years of friendship would do that, and she felt a sharp pang of fear that it could all be taken away if either she or Tate was fingered for Christie's murder.

When the frosting was finished, Mel covered the bowl with a damp cloth to keep it moist. It would be a few minutes until the cupcakes were cool enough to frost.

Angie and Tate resumed their seats at the table and began talking about what movies they wanted to watch on the next movie night. Angie was lobbying hard for an ac-

tion adventure night, but Tate was leaning towards a night
of independent films. A fierce feeling of protectiveness
swamped Mel as she watched them. These were her dear-
est friends, as close as you could get without sharing the
same parents. She wasn't going to let anyone or anything
harm them. Tomorrow, she would talk to Alma, and she'd
get some answers if she had to shake them out of her.

Mel remembered the address of Alma's apartment
from when she had looked her up to get her phone number.
Alma lived only a few miles away in a duplex in an old
neighborhood just on the east side of the park that ran the
length of Scottsdale, known locally as the green belt.

Mel sipped a paper cup full of strong coffee as she
wound through the neighborhood until she came to a squat,
yellow brick house that had a front door at each end of its
facade. Judging by the numbers, Alma's was the door on
the right.

Mel parked at the curb and strode towards the door. She
had come early, before she had to open the bakery, hoping
to catch Alma before she went out for the day.

There was no doorbell, so she rapped on the security
door with her knuckles. The heavy metal door hurt, so Mel
switched to the side of her fist.

She waited, expecting to see a face peer out of the window beside the door. There was nothing: no sound of anyone moving, no dog barking, nothing.

Maybe Alma couldn't hear her banging on the door. Mel
reached for the knob on the security door to see if it opened
so she could knock on the wooden door behind it. The knob
turned easily, and Mel gave the inner door a sharp rap with
her knuckles. In the morning quiet, it sounded like gunfire.
No one could sleep through that.

Except for maybe Alma, Mel thought, because there was still no answer.

"She's home."

Mel turned towards the voice. An older man, wearing a white T-shirt and plaid Bermuda shorts with a bright blue Chicago Cubs cap perched on his gray hair, was in the yard next door. He was unreeling his garden hose, but he paused to look Mel up and down.

"I heard her door slam late last night," he said. "It must have been about two in the morning. She's probably still sleeping it off."

"Oh." Mel wondered if she should knock again or come back later. Probably Alma wasn't going to hear the knock. She had to admit she'd get a certain satisfaction out of waking Alma up, given all the grief she'd been through. It'd be nice to share the pain. She tried the doorknob just to see if it turned. It did.

She glanced over at the neighbor, but he had turned his back to her and was watering his roses. Mel took a cautious step into the dark duplex and called, "Alma, it's Melanie Cooper. I need to talk to you."

The front door opened into a large living room. There were the requisite love seat and coffee table positioned in front of a flat-screen TV. In the corner was a large drawing table littered with sketches. An ashtray sat on the coffee table. A cigarette perched in the ashtray. It had burned down to the filter, obviously forgotten by whoever had lit it. Alma was lucky she hadn't torched the place.

The air in the apartment was stale and flavored with the musk of tobacco. Mel wrinkled her nose. It was then that she noticed the silence. It was too quiet in there, and the hair on the back of her neck prickled in alarm. Oh no, not again!

Mel hurried to the kitchen beyond. No one was there. A short hallway led to a bathroom (empty) and a bedroom.

Mel shoved the bedroom door open. She didn't care if she found Alma in bed with someone; in fact, she'd be delighted to find her so, given the panic that had just taken over her mind. But Alma wasn't in the bed, and neither was anyone else.

Alma was lying facedown on the floor, and she didn't appear to be breathing.

Nineteen

"Not again!" Mel cried as she raced across the messy bedroom, stepping over piles of discarded clothing to get to Alma.

She dropped to her knees and rolled the young woman over. Her black hair was greasy and plastered to her head by dried sweat. Her pale skin was even paler than usual, and Mel put her ear to her chest to see if she was breathing.

There was a very slight rise to her chest, and Mel reared back and stared at her. Had she just imagined it, or was Alma breathing? She couldn't tell. Panic made her fingers shake as she pressed them beneath Alma's ear, looking for a pulse. It was faint, but it was there.

"Alma," Mel called her name. "Alma, can you hear me?"

She forced open Alma's right eye and saw that the pupil was a tiny pinprick. At least she wasn't dead. Not yet.

Mel dug through her purse for her phone. She pulled it out, but it shut itself off because of a low battery. Damn it!

"Stay with me, Alma," she demanded, and ran out the front door.

The neighbor was still there, spraying his roses while sipping a steaming cup of coffee.

"Sir!" Mel yelled. "Sir, I found Alma. She's unconscious. Call 9-1-1."

"What?" The man looked at her in confusion. He released the sprayer nozzle and the water stopped. Mel repeated her order, and he gave a quick nod and barreled into his house.

Mel ran back to be beside Alma. She didn't want anything to happen to her. Not on her watch. Not this time.

In less than five minutes the sound of sirens filled the air. The neighbor led the EMTs into the house, and Mel quickly told them exactly what she'd found when she arrived: Alma, facedown and barely breathing.

They set to work trying to revive her while Mel stood beside the neighbor.

"Good thing for her you stopped by," he said. He looked distressed, and Mel patted his arm.

"Let's hope so," she said.

As the medics prepared to lift Alma onto a stretcher, her arm flopped down. One of the men, young with dark hair, leaned close to examine something on her side. He stood back and frowned at Mel.

"How well did you know her?" he asked.

"Not very," she said. "Why?"

"Did she have any conditions, like rheumatoid arthritis or a back injury, something that caused her constant pain?"

"I don't know," Mel said. "Why?"

"She's wearing a time-release pain patch," the medic said. "It's called fentanyl. It's an opiate that helps people in chronic pain."

"I don't know," Mel said again, feeling incredibly inadequate. She gave one of the medics her contact information and followed them out the door.

The neighbor offered to keep an eye on Alma's place, and when they found her address book by her drawing table, he said he'd contact her family in Texas.

"I met them once when they were out here for a visit," he said. "They seemed like nice folks."

"Thank you, Mr. . . ."

"Horowitz," he said. "But you can call me Ben."

They shook hands and Mel climbed into her car, feeling like she just stepped off the Tilt-O-Whirl at the Arizona State Fair and hadn't gotten her balance back.

This was no accident. Someone had tried to kill Alma. But who? Terry Longmore seemed the likely candidate. Maybe Alma was getting too demanding in her new job. Maybe she had too much leverage over him, given that they had stolen a gown and possibly murdered Christie together.

There was something about the pain patch that bothered her, however. She couldn't help thinking it was a pivotal piece to the puzzle, but she couldn't make it fit.

She drove down Hayden Road with the windows down. She was on autopilot, stopping or slowing at traffic lights, but she couldn't have said whether they were green or red or yellow. Her brain whirred like an old hard drive trying to load too much information.

The photographer. Her memory of talking to Jay Driscoll came into her brain in a rush. He had said something about weight-loss patches at the photo shoot.

What had he said? Oh yeah, that they'd been delayed because Christie and her assistant had to put on some patch.

She turned right on Camelback Road and wound her way through Old Town. She found a parking spot on Main Street and hurried into the bakery. Angie was in back, getting ready to open.

Mel ran past her to the office.

"Well, hello to you, too," Angie said.

Mel grabbed the cordless phone in the office and punched in Uncle Stan's number.

"Cooper here," he answered on the third ring.

"Does the ME know what killed Christie yet?"

"Melanie?" he said.

"Yes, it's me. This is important. Have they figured it out yet?"

"I'm out of the loop on that case," he said. "And I can't talk to you about it."

"Tell them to check for an opiate," Mel said. "Something that would be time-released in a pain patch."

"What's going on, Mel?" His low voice was a bark.

"I went to see Alma Rodriguez today," Mel said. "I found her unconscious. She was unresponsive but alive. The medic said she had a pain patch on and wanted to know if she had any chronic conditions. I don't think she did. Uncle Stan, I think whoever murdered Christie tried to murder Alma, too."

"I'll call you back," he said, and hung up.

Angie was standing in the door, looking stunned.

"You heard?" Mel asked.

"All of it," she said. "Who would want Alma dead?"

"The killer," Mel said.

Angie slumped into the chair beside Mel's desk.

"You think Alma knew who the killer was?"

"I don't know," Mel said. The phone rang, and she picked it up. "Hello."

"I talked to the ME," Uncle Stan said. "They don't generally check for substances like that in their initial tox screen. They're going to run it now."

"Let me know what they find out," Mel said.

Uncle Stan let out a sigh. "Mel, I'm calling your mother.

I don't want you to leave the bakery until we know what's going on."

"Don't," she said. "She'll just worry."

"Good, then she can join me," he retorted. "I'm not kidding, Melanie Jean Cooper, you do not set one toe outside of that bakery. There's a killer on the loose, and now that you've stopped them by finding Alma, you could very well be the next target. I'm sending a squad car to park out front. Do not move!"

He hung up before Mel could offer further arguments. She glanced at her watch. If Uncle Stan called her mother, then she had precisely four and a half minutes to get out of there before she was trapped.

She grabbed her purse and her phone charger out of the top desk drawer.

"Where are you going?" Angie asked.

"Serenity Springs," she said.

"Where Olivia's mother is? Why?"

"This is going to sound crazy," Mel said as she hurried around the desk.

"Try me," Angie said.

"What if Olivia murdered Christie?" Mel asked. She glanced over her shoulder to see Angie's reaction, and bumped into the door frame. "Ouch."

"'Yes, we've made quite a few changes around here since you went crazy,'" Angie quipped.

Mel paused and grinned. "*Pink Panther* with Peter Sellers. Very nice."

Angie ducked her head in humble acknowledgment. "Um, seriously, that's nuts. Why would Olivia murder Christie? She didn't even know her."

"Think about it," Mel said, leading the way into the kitchen. "Olivia has been obsessed with watching us. She's completely paranoid that Fairy Tale Cupcakes will run her out of business. Tate and Christie's wedding was going to be the event of the year, and we were hired to provide the cupcakes. What better way to make sure that didn't happen than to kill the bride?"

"I know Olivia is crackers, but still, that's whacktacular even for her."

"Is it?" Mel asked. "I was there when she went mental on the attendant. What if she was making a scene to cover her tracks? What if she was stealing her mother's pain meds and used them on Christie?"

"Even if she did murder Christie, why would she go after Alma?"

"I don't know. Maybe Alma figured it out," Mel said.

"How would Olivia have gotten close to Christie?" Angie asked.

"I don't know, but I'm going to Serenity Springs, and I'm going to find that attendant and ask him if it's possible that Olivia is really the one stealing the medication."

"Your mother and Uncle Stan are going to have fits," Angie said. "I'll come with you."

"No. I need you here, in case any more information comes in about what killed Christie. I promise I'll charge my phone in the car and be in constant contact."

"Call me every fifteen minutes, or I'm coming after you," Angie said. She crossed the room and glanced out the window. "Your mother's car just pulled up. You'd better go out the back. I'll stall her."

"Thanks, Angie." Mel gave her a quick squeeze as she hustled out the back.

"Fifteen minutes!" Angie called after her.

Mel hurried around the side of the building. She waited until her mother entered the shop and then bolted for her car. It was time for her and Olivia to have their final showdown, and Mel was going to be ready.

Twenty

Olivia's pink van wasn't in the parking lot when Mel pulled into Serenity Springs. Good. Mel was hoping to have a minute to track down the attendant Olivia had been verbally abusing.

If what Mel suspected was true, then the young man would probably be happy to tell her that the real thief was Olivia, and if the ME found what Mel suspected, then the evidence around Olivia would become incontrovertible.

The sliding doors opened when she stepped on the black rubber mat. The same young woman who had been at the reception desk was there again. Mel scanned her memory for the girl's name. Grace, that was it.

Today, she was wearing a navy blue sheath dress embroidered with white flowers. As soon as she saw Mel, she smiled in recognition and Mel felt as if she had been hugged. No wonder they had her working the front desk; she probably made everyone coming to see their elderly relative feel better.

Mel imagined the decision to put a parent in assisted care was a heavy one, and Grace's smile made it seem okay.

"Ms. McAllister, it's nice to see you again," she gushed.

Mel debated telling her the truth about who she was, but feared it might make things overly complicated.

"Hi, Grace," she said.

Grace frowned at her. "Are you here to see Ms. Puckett? I'm afraid she hasn't been in to see her mother yet."

"Actually, I have another story I'm working on," Mel said. "It's about elder care and prescription drugs."

Grace gave her a cautious look. "I'd have to refer you to our director for any information about that."

"That's fine," Mel said. She watched as Grace flipped through a phone list. "When I was here the other day, I heard Olivia yelling at someone about her mother's medication. That's what gave me the idea. It seemed to me that the poor guy was being wrongly accused, and I wondered if that happens often."

Grace's head snapped up. Her bright blue eyes sparked. "I'll say it does."

Mel knew she had chosen the right angle to work when Grace lowered her voice and said, "Honestly, it's usually a member of the family."

"Really?"

The doors behind them opened, and a resident in a wheelchair was pushed in by an orderly. They nodded as they passed, and Grace hurried around the desk, gesturing for Mel to follow her.

"I'd be in big trouble if they knew I told you this," she said. "But if you keep my name out of it, I can tell you that in Mrs. Puckett's case, we finally put a security camera in her room to try to catch the thief."

Mel felt her body slow down with a whoosh. This was

it. Olivia was going to be caught, and she and Tate would finally be free from suspicion.

"So, did you catch her, er, the person?"

"Unfortunately, no," Grace said. "There were technical difficulties, but they're going to try again."

"Do you think they'll catch Olivia soon, then?" Mel asked with what she knew was ill-concealed impatience.

"Olivia?" Grace blinked at her. "They're not going after Olivia, they're trying to catch her niece, Phoebe."

"Phoebe?" Mel asked. She felt the rush of adrenaline slam through her again. "She's about this tall, long blonde hair, dresses in bright colors, and giggles a lot."

"That's her," Grace said with a scowl. "Her aunt's been covering for her, but we suspected her from the beginning."

Mel grabbed Grace's arm and squeezed. "Thank you so much. You've been great, just great."

She dashed out of the facility with Grace yelling, "You're welcome!" after her.

She was just outside the door when she paused to call Angie. She flipped her phone open and got into her contacts. She quickly picked Angie and waited while the phone dialed.

Angie picked up on the first ring.

"What's the good word?"

"It's not who I thought," Mel said.

"Is that Melanie?"

Mel could hear her mother's voice in the background.

"Tell her to get back here right now."

That was not her mother's voice. It was much too deep and commanding, like Joe.

"Who's there with you?" she asked.

"It'd be shorter to tell you who isn't here," Angie said. She sounded beleaguered.

"Tell everyone I'm fine," Mel said. "I'll call back when I can."

"Wait!" Angie said. "Tell me what's happening."

"I can't," Mel said. "I don't want anyone to interfere. I'll call when I can."

She shut her phone and climbed into her Mini Cooper. She had just turned the key in the ignition when she felt something hard press against the base of her skull.

"Did you really think I wouldn't find out what you were doing?" Phoebe said as she popped up behind her.

"Phoebe, what a surprise," Mel said. She tried to sound casual but with a lethal-looking gun pointed at the back of her head, her voice gave way, making her sound almost as terrified as she felt.

"Drive," Phoebe said. "I think we'll go pay my aunt a visit."

"Who's your aunt?" Mel asked, hoping that playing dumb bought her some time and maybe some backup.

"Really?" Phoebe said with a shake of her blonde pony-tail. "Is that really how you want to play it? I expected more out of you."

"Sorry to disappoint," Mel said. Her eyes scanned the parking lot for help. There was no one. She glanced back in the mirror and met Phoebe's gaze. Had she really never noticed the crazy glint in her eyes? That'd teach her.

"I'm sure you are." Phoebe grinned. But it wasn't a happy look; instead, it made Mel feel as if icy fingers had reached into her chest to squeeze her heart.

"Drive," Phoebe said. "And just so we don't have to play your little 'duh' game again, yes, our destination is Confections."

Mel pulled out of the parking lot with Phoebe the time bomb in the backseat. What would detonate her finger on the trigger? A speed bump? A careless turn? Mel had no idea.

Why hadn't she told Angie where she was going? Oh, yeah, she didn't want anyone to interfere. Ha! That was a laugh riot now, wasn't it? How arrogant she'd been to think she could take on a stone-cold killer by herself.

Mel thought of her mother and how she had suffered when her father died. She desperately did not want to put Joyce through that again. She thought about her brother, Charlie. He'd been calling her to see if she was okay, and she'd given him the brush-off, not wanting to worry him. Now, she'd give anything to be on the phone with him—not just to have him call the police for her, but so she could tell him how much she loved him and what a good brother he'd always been.

She felt her throat get tight, but swallowed past the lump. She glanced in the mirror and saw Phoebe watching her with a small smile of satisfaction. She was enjoying this, she was enjoying Mel's angst and pain. Something snapped inside Mel. She refused to go out sad and maudlin. No, if she was going, she was going pissed and was planning to take Phoebe with her.

"What's the matter?" Phoebe purred. "Are you getting annoyed with me?"

Mel glanced back at the road. She wasn't going to give her the satisfaction of seeing her anger. She compressed her lips into a thin line, tried not to think about the gun pointed at her head, and made the two left turns and one right turn that led them into the Confections parking lot.

It was still early, too early for Confections to be open. Phoebe led Mel out of the car towards the front door. She banged on the glass with three short raps.

The vertical blinds moved, and an eye stared out at them. Mel would have known that eye anywhere. Olivia.

The blinds went back into place, and with several turns and clicks the door was unlocked and pushed open towards them.

Phoebe gave Mel a shove that pushed her over the threshold and into the bakery.

"What are you doing here?" Olivia snapped at Mel.

Her gray corkscrew hair was twisted up onto her head and her cheeks were flushed in anger. She glanced behind Mel as if she wanted to shield her display cases from Mel's prying eyes.

"Don't worry, you have bigger problems than me making off with one of your cookie recipes," Mel said.

"Phoebe, why are you with *her*?" Olivia asked.

"She's a present," Phoebe said. "Forgive me, I didn't have time to wrap her."

"What are you talking about?" Olivia glanced between them.

"Is anyone else here?" Phoebe asked.

"No, it's just me until ten o'clock," Olivia said. "Now, really, what is this all about?"

"Your niece is a killer," Mel said. "Didn't you know?"

"My niece? Ha!" Olivia barked. "Don't tell me you're trying to frame her to get to me."

Mel shook her head. Obviously, the crazy apple had not rolled far from the crazy tree.

"She didn't frame me," Phoebe said. "And unfortunately, my attempts to frame her have failed."

"Frame her?" Olivia leaned against her display case as if she needed the support. "What are you talking about?"

"Oh, come on, Auntie, surely you must have suspected," Phoebe said. At Olivia's blank stare, Phoebe turned to Mel and said, "She's not the brightest, but she does make a mean snickerdoodle."

Phoebe turned back to Olivia and pulled the gun out from behind her back. "I killed Christie Stevens."

"No!" Olivia gasped.

" 'Fraid so."

"But you adored her," Olivia protested. "You always said she was a visionary."

"Yeah, well, she was also a coldhearted bitch, and believe me, it takes one to know one."

Olivia slapped a hand over her chest and staggered back. Mel's eyes widened at this little bit of melodrama.

"Are you really trying to convince me that you didn't know Phoebe was stealing your mother's pain patches, and that she used one to kill Christie?"

"Huh." Phoebe tapped her chin with the forefinger of the hand not holding the gun. "You're smarter than you look, Blondie."

"You were stealing Mother's pain patches?" Olivia gaped. "Phoebe, how could you?"

"I had a problem that I needed to take care of," Phoebe said. "Remember the safety lesson that the nurse gave us on how to put the patches on Nana? She was very clear that fentanyl is deadly if too much is administered. Not for someone like Nana, who has developed such a high tolerance, but for someone like Christie it wouldn't take much at all. Well, it got me to thinking. Then I did a little checking, and it turns out that the ME rarely checks for the drug fentanyl in a tox screen, so I knew that would be the perfect way to get rid of Christie. Well, that and planting a little rat poison in one of your cupcakes to send the trail of bread crumbs in your direction, thus nailing two birds with one stone, as they say."

"It didn't quite work out, though, did it?" Mel asked.

"No," Phoebe said. "Best laid plans and all that. I tried to break into your shop and plant some of the rat poison I put in the cupcake, but that adorable DA was there with you, and I had to bail."

"That was *you* watching my apartment that night," Mel said. "I knew I saw someone."

"Phoebe, I don't understand." Olivia's voice was a whimper. "Why would you murder your boss, and what does *she* have to do with it?"

"Christie had me locked up in a contract tighter than Madonna in a bustier," Phoebe said. "I couldn't get out, and believe me I wanted out. I was fielding offers from design houses in Paris and Milan. She stole everything from me. But the final straw was the wedding gown. She promised me that if I designed it for her, she'd give me full credit, but she lied.

"I heard her talking to Jay Driscoll at the photo shoot, and she told him that *Vogue* and *Harper's Bazaar* were in a bidding war over who would run a feature of her in the gown she designed for her own wedding. I stuck the patch on her that very night. Then I saw the cupcakes you sent over, and I realized if I framed you for it, I'd be helping out Auntie, too, by killing off her competition. Perfect, yes?"

"Phoebe, that's just sick!" Olivia cried. "Surely you didn't think you'd actually get away with it?"

"Oh, I'll get away with it," Phoebe said. She walked behind the counter and helped herself to a ribbon cookie. She nibbled on it and then glared at her aunt. "And you, Auntie, are going to help me."

"Of course, I'll get help for you," Olivia said, and took a step towards Phoebe.

Phoebe raised the gun, and Olivia halted, finding herself nose to gun barrel. She swallowed, and a sheen of sweat glistened on her forehead.

Mel knew she needed to distract Phoebe before she did something really crazy, like pull the trigger.

"What about Alma? Why did you go after her?"

Phoebe turned to face Mel and stepped away from Olivia.

"That's your fault," she said.

"How do you figure?" Mel asked.

"Don't you remember?" Phoebe asked. "You're the one who told me that she took the gown and exchanged it for a job with Terry Longmore, the hack. *My gown.* She took *my gown.* That design was going to be my entrée onto the international scene. I had to get it back. Plus, I knew she suspected I was the killer, so I had to cover my ass."

"She didn't die," Mel said. "I found her in time. In fact, it was finding her with the patch on that made me put it all together. She's going to wake up and talk, and you're going to be busted not only for murder but for attempted murder as well."

"That's unfortunate," Phoebe said. "Oh, not that I'm going to jail, because I'm not, but rather that Alma lived. But I think I planted enough pain patches in her apartment to be sure that she goes away for a very long time. After all, who's a judge going to believe, a crazy junkie murderer or me?"

She batted her big, blue eyes, and Mel felt herself tremble. Phoebe was beyond crazy and well into deranged. She glanced at Olivia, and was not reassured to see her own horrified expression mirrored back at her.

"So, shall we?" Phoebe said.

"Shall we what?" Olivia asked.

Phoebe gestured at Mel with the gun. "Dispose of her."

Olivia pulled herself off the display case. She sucked in a deep breath and said, "No, Phoebe, I won't be a party to murder."

Mel found herself more than a little surprised. Frankly, she had thought Olivia would jump at the chance to be rid of her competition.

"Very well, then." Phoebe shook the gun at them and gestured for them to walk toward the back of the shop. "I see I'm on my own."

"Phoebe." Olivia's voice held a note of fear. "What are you going to do?"

"Looks like you two are going to die in a rivalry gone wrong," Phoebe said. "Good thing I had Christie's father put all those flyers about you being a murderer all over Old Town, Mel. That'll certainly make it believable."

"Christie's father did that?" Mel asked.

"Genius, I know," Phoebe said. "He hired some teenagers to do it, but I bet he keeps quiet and lets Auntie take the rap."

"Phoebe, your mother was my sister," Olivia said in a plaintive voice. "You have to know she would never want you to harm me."

"Truth be told," Phoebe said, "she didn't like you very much. She thought you were pretty bossy. She was right."

She led them to a walk-in cooler and gestured them inside. Once the door was shut, she pushed a steel worktable in front of it.

"I just need a few minutes to think," Phoebe said. "You two just chill, and I'll be back. Get it, chill?"

They heard her laughing as she walked away.

"This is all your fault!" Olivia rounded on Mel.

"My fault?" Mel yelled back. "You have a psychotic murdering niece, and that's my fault?"

"If you hadn't opened up your stupid little cupcake shop, neither of us would be in this mess right now."

"There's some logic for you," Mel snapped. "How about we save the argument and try to figure out a way out of this?"

"What are we going to do, egg her?" Olivia asked sarcastically as she examined the supplies on the shelves.

"Puckett," Mel said, "I like the way you're thinking."

Twenty-one

"How good is your aim?" Olivia asked.

"We've got five dozen eggs here," Mel said. "How good does it have to be?"

"Aim for the eyes," Olivia said. "If you blind her, I can get the gun."

"Do you really think it's loaded?" Mel asked.

The hum of the cooler was the only sound while Olivia sucked in her cheeks to consider Mel's question.

"She once took her father's pride and joy, a '65 Mustang convertible, for a joy ride when he specifically told her no. When he found out and took away her keys, she just glared at him. Two days later the car was stolen. When they found it in the desert, it had been keyed, red paint had been dumped on the leather interior, and it had been set on fire. Her father always suspected that Phoebe did it as revenge. My sister, her mother, refused to believe it. Either way, Phoebe never admitted it. There were other things like that, but my sister always covered for her. It cost her the marriage. Phoebe's father finally got fed up and left."

"She's a sociopath," Mel said.

Olivia sighed. "We thought she was just a brat. I never expected anything like this, but am I surprised? Ultimately, no."

Mel looked at the crate of eggs in front of her. Her aim had better be damn straight, because she had a feeling that gun was indeed loaded.

It seemed like hours passed before Phoebe came back. Mel felt the cold seep into her bones, and her teeth began to chatter. She remembered just weeks ago when her mother had "accidentally" shut Tate and her in the walk-in at the cupcake shop. She'd give anything to be there now with him, instead of here with Olivia.

Finally, they heard the sound of the steel table being dragged away, and Phoebe yelled through the door.

"Put your hands on your heads, and walk out nice and slow."

"This is it," Olivia whispered. "Are you ready?"

"Just duck on three," Mel said.

She quickly palmed two eggs and held them just out of view behind her head as the door swung wide. Phoebe stood in the light, pointing the gun right at them.

"One, two, three," Mel hissed and Olivia dropped down as Mel fired both eggs right at Phoebe's face.

There was a satisfying crack followed by a shriek. Olivia darted out of the cooler and grabbed Phoebe's gun hand as Mel bent down and began lobbing eggs at Phoebe for all she was worth.

Olivia tried banging Phoebe's hand against the table, but Phoebe didn't let go. She was dripping egg yolks, and bits of shell were in her hair and on her clothes as Mel pelted her with eggs. Phoebe hauled back with her left fist as if she would punch her aunt, but the egg-slick floor caused her to slip, and she went down hard, with Olivia landing on top of her.

"Help!" Olivia yelled as she tried to keep ahold on Phoebe, but the younger woman was wiggling out of her grasp.

Mel didn't hesitate. She jumped into the fray, sliding on the linoleum floor and falling with a bone-jarring crack on her rump. She scrambled to her knees and reached out to grab the gun just as Olivia was losing her grip on Phoebe's wrist. Mel tossed the gun across the room and grabbed Phoebe's arms.

"Trap her legs!" Mel yelled. Olivia heaved herself off the slippery floor like a walrus lumbering out of the sea and dropped on top of her niece.

Just then the kitchen door slammed open, and Uncle Stan and Joe DeLaura jumped into the room. Uncle Stan leveled a gun in their direction and yelled, "Freeze! Nobody move!"

"Uh." Phoebe raised her head and then plopped it back into the egg yuck on the floor. Mel and Olivia exchanged a slippery high five before they rolled off Phoebe in exhausted relief.

\'.\'\

"How, exactly, did Uncle Stan find me?" Mel asked.

Angie looked sheepish. "I had my brother Tony track your cell phone."

"I take it you're speaking to him and Sal again?"

"For now," Angie agreed. "When you didn't call back within fifteen minutes, I panicked."

"Good call," Mel said. "I ran out of eggs right as Uncle Stan and Joe barged in."

"'So it was a real 'wakey, wakey, eggs and bakey' moment,'" Tate said.

"*Kill Bill 2*." Angie identified the quote. "Nice."

"Thanks. I've been waiting to use that one," he said.

"Happy I could help," Mel said as she draped the towel she'd been using on her hair around her neck.

After she had given her statement and answered all of the detectives' questions, she had been sent home to deal with the raw egg that had dried in her hair. On the upside, her hair was silky smooth and shiny, and on the downside, it had taken three shampoos to get it all out.

Her mother had left, after three cycles of hugging her and crying, to go call Mel's brother with the good news. Uncle Stan had gone to the station to oversee Phoebe being taken into custody, even though it was no longer his case. With Olivia's statement and Mel's, Joe felt it was very unlikely that Phoebe would be seeing daylight anytime soon, which suited Mel just fine.

Since business had been slow all evening, Tate and Angie had decided to take a dinner break and were sitting at the steel table in the kitchen with several Chinese takeout boxes surrounding them. They had ordered in Mel's favorite, and she was just getting ready to dig in when there was a knock on the back door.

"Rule of closeness," Angie said.

"But I had a near-death experience today," Mel protested. "I think I should get a pass even if I am closest to the door."

Tate and Angie exchanged a look. "Nah."

"Fine," Mel huffed. She strode to the door and threw it wide.

Standing there was Joe. He smiled at her, and she desperately wished she had taken the time to get dressed instead of wearing her flannel bathrobe with the cows all over it.

"Hi," he said.

"Hi," she repeated stupidly.

"Can I talk to you?"

"Sure, what is it?" Then she had a panicked thought. "They're not going to let her out are they? She killed Christie. She admitted it. Olivia will back me up."

"No," he said. "It's nothing like that."

"Oh." Mel sagged with relief.

He caught her by the ends of the towel still draped around her neck. He pulled her close and kissed her.

For twenty-plus years, Melanie Cooper had wondered what it would be like to be kissed by Joe DeLaura, and now she knew . . . it was . . . amazing.

He pulled back to look at her, and Mel felt her face get hot.

"Wow."

"And how," he said.

"What made you do that?" she asked.

"I've wanted to for a while now," he said. "And since you're no longer a suspect, I figured now was my chance."

"Ah," she said.

"Truthfully," he continued, "I haven't been able to get you out of my mind since the day I came over to review that contract for you. I'd have asked you out even if you were on your way to jail."

Mel grinned. "So, you're asking me out?"

"How does dinner and a movie sound?"

"What about what's-her-name, your associate?" Mel asked.

"Just business," he said. "Believe me, everyone else seems pretty boring when you're around, Cupcake."

Cupcake? She knew that as a female entrepreneur, she shouldn't let him get away with calling her such a frivolous nickname. But darn it, it made her feel breathless the way he said it in his low voice accompanied by his slow grin. And she liked it.

"Speaking of business," he said, "did you know that

there's a big pink van parked in front of your building?"

"A pink what?" Mel asked, stepping back from him.

"Van," he said. "It's right out front."

Mel spun on her heel and stomped back into the kitchen, where Angie and Tate were still sitting.

"How's business been tonight?" she asked.

Angie was fishing in a carton with a pair of chopsticks, and Tate had a mouthful. They exchanged a look that said they didn't want to tell her.

"Dead," Angie admitted reluctantly.

"Do you think it could be because Olivia's back?" Mel asked.

"What?" They both jumped from their seats and followed Mel into the main room, which was forlornly empty of customers.

Mel opened the front door, and sure enough, there was Olivia's big pink van parked in front of their shop. With an enormous tray full of cookies, Olivia was walking back and forth in front of Fairy Tale Cupcakes, offering free cookies to anyone who happened by.

"Are you kidding me?" Mel yelled. "I saved your miserable life, and you're still trying to run me out of business!"

"*You* saved *my* life?" Olivia asked. "Ha! *I* saved *your* life! The way I see it, you owe me one, and I'll take all of your customers as payback."

"That's it!" Mel was about to launch herself at Olivia when an arm looped around her waist, pulling her back. She glanced over her shoulder and gave Joe her best glare, but his grip didn't slacken a bit.

Angie had been hot on her heels, but Tate had snatched her in the same around-the-middle grab before her feet left the curb.

"You'd better move this van, ma'am," Joe said. "I don't know how much longer we can hold 'em."

Angie let loose a feral snarl, and Olivia's eyes went wide. She hustled her cookies and herself into the van and quickly pulled away.

As the pink van banged into the curb in Olivia's haste to vacate the premises, Mel felt a laugh bubble up from somewhere down deep. Joe looked at her like he was worried that she was cracking up, but then the ridiculousness of the situation seemed to strike him as well, and he began to laugh, too.

Tate and Angie soon joined in, and it turned into a chorus of giggles and guffaws. That's when Mel knew that everything was going to be okay. Yes, she saw Angie look at Tate with a love in her eyes that he was unaware of. And yes, Tate's eyes were shadowed by the betrayal and death of his fiancée. But the three of them were still here and still together, and now Joe was with them, too. For Mel, right now was the only moment that mattered.

Recipes

Blonde Bombshell

An almond-flavored cupcake topped with vanilla buttercream and sprinkled with toasted almonds.

¾ cup unsalted butter, softened
1½ cups sugar
2 eggs, at room temperature
1½ teaspoons almond extract
½ teaspoon vanilla extract
2½ teaspoons baking powder
¼ teaspoon salt
2½ cups flour
1 ¼ cups milk

Preheat oven to 350 degrees. Sift together flour, baking powder, and salt. Set aside. Cream butter and sugar at medium speed, add eggs and milk, and beat until smooth. Beat in extracts. Add dry ingredients, beat until smooth. Fill cupcake liners ⅔ full. Bake until golden brown, about 20 minutes. Makes 24.

Frost with vanilla buttercream and sprinkle with toasted almond slivers.

Toasted almonds: Preheat oven to 350 degrees. Spread nuts in one layer on an ungreased, shallow baking pan. Bake for 10 to 15 minutes, stirring occasionally, until golden.

Buttercream Frosting

½ cup solid vegetable shortening
½ cup (1 stick) butter or margarine, softened
1 teaspoon clear vanilla extract
4 cups sifted confectioners' sugar
2 tablespoons milk

In large bowl, cream shortening and butter. Add vanilla. Gradually add sugar, one cup at a time, beating well on medium speed. Scrape sides of bowl often. Add milk, and beat at medium speed until light and fluffy. Keep bowl covered with a damp cloth until ready to use. Makes 3 cups of icing.

Tinkerbells

Lemon cupcakes with raspberry buttercream
frosting rolled in pink sugar.

1 cup (2 sticks) unsalted butter, softened
2 cups granulated sugar, divided
4 extra-large eggs, at room temperature
⅓ cup grated lemon zest (6 to 8 large lemons)
3 cups flour
½ teaspoon baking powder
½ teaspoon baking soda
1 teaspoon salt
¼ cup freshly squeezed lemon juice
¾ cup buttermilk, at room temperature
1 teaspoon pure vanilla extract

Preheat the oven to 350 degrees. Cream the butter and 2
cups granulated sugar until fluffy, about 5 minutes. With
the mixer on medium speed, add the eggs, one at a time,
and the lemon zest. Sift together the flour, baking powder,
baking soda, and salt in a bowl. In another bowl, combine
the lemon juice, buttermilk, and vanilla. Add the flour and
buttermilk mixtures alternately to the batter, beginning
and ending with the flour. Use an ice cream scoop to fill
paper-lined cupcake pan. Bake 20 minutes. Makes 24.

Raspberry Buttercream

Use previous buttercream recipe, but instead of milk and
vanilla, use a half cup of fresh raspberries. Be sure to wash
and dry raspberries thoroughly before mixing them in.
Roll the cupcakes in pink decorating sugar before the buttercream has set.

Mojito

A dense, golden cupcake flavored with lime zest
and dried mint leaves, and topped with a
rum-flavored icing.

½ cup sugar
1½ cups flour
¼ teaspoon salt
2 teaspoons baking powder
¼ cup melted butter
1 beaten egg
1 cup milk
1 lime, juice and zest
2 teaspoons dried spearmint leaves

Preheat the oven to 350 degrees. Sift the dry ingredients together in a big bowl. Melt the butter and add the beaten egg
to it. Add that to the dry ingredients, then stir in the milk
until smooth. Zest half of a lime, and add it to the bowl.
Squeeze in the juice of half the lime as well. Add the dried
spearmint leaves to the batter, mixing well. Bake for 16-20
minutes or until it springs back to the touch. Makes 12.

Rum-Flavored Buttercream Frosting

Use previous buttercream recipe but substitute rum extract
for vanilla. Garnish with candied spearmint leaf, fresh
mint leaf, or lime wedge.

Death by Chocolate

Dark chocolate ganache on a chocolate with
chocolate chips cupcake.

> *1¹/₃ cups all-purpose flour*
> *2 teaspoons baking powder*
> *¼ teaspoon baking soda*
> *¾ cup unsweetened cocoa powder*
> *⅛ teaspoon salt*
> *3 tablespoons butter, softened*
> *1½ cups white sugar*
> *2 eggs, at room temperature*
> *¾ teaspoon vanilla extract*
> *1 cup milk*
> *1 bag semisweet chocolate chips*

Preheat oven to 350 degrees. Sift together the flour, baking powder, baking soda, cocoa, and salt. Set aside. In a large bowl, cream together the butter and sugar until well blended. Add the eggs one at a time, beating well with each addition, then stir in the vanilla. Add the flour mixture alternately with the milk; beat well. Add the chocolate chips. Bake for 15 to 17 minutes. Makes 12.

Dark Chocolate Ganache

> *2 cups dark chocolate chips*
> *2 cups heavy cream*
> *2 teaspoons vanilla extract*

Place chocolate chips in a large bowl. Pour the cream into a saucepan, and bring it to a boil. Once the cream boils, remove it from the heat and pour it over the chips. Let stand for a minute or two, then stir with a whisk until smooth. Be sure to scrape the bottom of the bowl occasionally. Stir in the vanilla until well blended. Place a piece of plastic wrap directly on the surface of the ganache and allow it to cool to room temperature. Dip tops of cool cupcakes into the mixture and allow it to dry.

Turn the page for a preview of the next book
in the Cupcake Bakery Mysteries
by Jenn McKinlay . . .

Buttercream Bump Off

Available from Berkley Prime Crime!

"You need to get to the corner of Fifth and Scotts-dale. Now."

"Angie?" Melanie Cooper barely recognized her business partner's voice through her sleep induced haze. "What's going on?"

"Fifth and Scottsdale," Angie repeated. The phone went dead.

Mel glanced at the cell phone in her hand then at her alarm clock which read six fifty-seven. A phone call this early in the morning had better mean Angie's car was on fire or worse.

She heaved her comforter off and rolled out of the bed. Mel didn't like mornings on the best of days, but in January, even in Scottsdale, Arizona, it was surely a crime to be dragged out of bed before the sun, especially without a cup of coffee to chase away the morning chill. Still, Angie was her best friend going on twenty plus years. She wouldn't have called if it wasn't important.

That thought got Mel moving. She grabbed a thick hooded sweatshirt and tugged it on over her flannel pajamas. She could feel the static raise her short blonde hair up and she imagined she looked like a troll doll on a bad hair day, without the cute belly button showing. She jammed her feet into her slip-on sneakers and grabbed her keys.

Mel lived in a snug studio apartment above her cupcake bakery, Fairy Tale Cupcakes, in the heart of Old Town Scottsdale. Angie DeLaura was her partner, along with their other childhood friend Tate Harper, who was their main investor. Fifth and Scottsdale was only a block away. She could be there in minutes.

She pounded down the back stairs and hurried to her red Mini Cooper, which was parked in an adjacent lot. Two quick rights and she slid into a parking spot in front of an art gallery. The commuter traffic was just beginning and the light at the corner had an impressive line of cars waiting for it to change. Mel spotted Angie sitting on a wooden bench just south of the corner.

She didn't appear to be sporting burns or lacerations, so a car accident was out of the question.

"What's up?" Mel asked as she slid onto the bench beside her.

"Wait for it," Angie said and handed her a large, steaming latte in a tall paper cup.

Ah, Mel's will to live increased tenfold.

"Wait for . . . ?"

Angie held up her hand and Mel took a sip from her cup, knowing it would do no good to press. Angie was stubborn like that.

The steaming swallow of coffee was halfway down her throat, when she glanced up and saw a six-foot-tall cupcake come around the corner, approaching the crosswalk. Her coffee shot back up her throat and she erupted into a fit of coughing, causing Angie to pound her on the back.

Mel shoved her aside as soon as she could drag in a breath and goggled at the enormous pink confection strutting between the idling vehicles. It only took a moment to recognize her arch enemy, but there was no doubt. The cupcake was Olivia Puckett!

She was wearing a blue satin skirt, pleated accordion style and topped by a pink puffy blouse, stuffed to resemble frosting and beaded to give it a sprinkle effect. She wore this over bright blue support hose and broad white high heels. She also had a big round cherry on top of her head tied under her chin like a bonnet. She was handing out bright pink flyers, one of which Angie shoved into Mel's hands.

"Free Cupcakes!" it read in bold print. It was a coupon to anyone who entered Confections, Olivia's rival bakery.

"Do you think it's a felony to hit a cupcake with your car?" Mel asked.

"Hard to say, you might want to check with Uncle Stan first," Angie said.

Mel's uncle Stan was a detective in the Scottsdale Police Department. She supposed she could ask, but somehow she didn't think she'd like the answer.

The light changed and they watched as the enormous cupcake was caught in the crosswalk and had to hustle her pleated derriere out of the way before the rude honks escalated to rude hand gestures.

It was then, as she tottered on the curb, trying to catch her balance, that the giant cupcake spotted Angie and Mel. She gave them a calculated glance as if she considered them potential customers but then recognition kicked in. Her ingratiating smile morphed into a look of haughty disdain, impressive with a cherry the size of a bowling ball on her head, and she turned away from them with her nose in the air.

"You'd think after her shenanigans last year, Olivia would strive to maintain a lower profile," Angie said.

"You'd think," Mel agreed. "But what kind of nemesis would she be if she crawled off and disappeared?"

"True," Angie said. "Where would we channel all of our misdirected rage if we didn't have Ginormica Cupcake?"

A honk blared and Mel glanced up in time to see a silver Lexus pass by Olivia, who dropped her basket in surprise. The Lexus zoomed away and Mel recognized the driver as Tate, their business partner. Before she could retrieve her basket, Olivia's bright pink coupons were jettisoned by a blast of exhaust from a passing Escalade and it looked like an impromptu ticker tape parade.

Mel felt Angie nudge her when a motorcycle cop with his lights flashing pulled up alongside the giant cupcake. Over the roar of traffic, it was impossible to hear the conversation but judging by Olivia's wild hand gestures and bobbing cherry hat, it wasn't going her way.

Just then Tate pulled up beside them and said, " 'What we're dealing with here is a complete lack of respect for the law.' "

"*Smokey and the Bandit*?" Mel asked. "You're quoting Buford T. Justice from *Smokey and the Bandit*?"

"It's a classic," Tate said as he pushed open the passenger door.

Mel glanced up and saw Olivia gesturing wildly in their direction. The police officer was studying them over the top of his sunglasses.

"We can debate what merits a classic movie later," Angie said and gave Mel a shove into the car. "Get in! Put your pedal to the floor, Bandit!"

Tate stepped on the gas and they shot out into the traffic. Mel and Angie smiled and waved as they passed Olivia while the officer scribbled a citation on his pad and tore it off and handed it to Olivia with a flourish. She looked ready to spit sprinkles at them and Mel sank back into her seat, clutching her latte with a smile.

"Well, that was worth getting up before the sun," she said.

Tate circled the block and parked in front of Fairy Tale Cupcakes.

He opened the car doors for Angie and Mel and said, "Probably, we should wait before we go get your cars."

"We'll get them later," Mel said. "I have to prep for my couples' cooking club tonight."

"Ah, yes, your lead-up to Valentine's Day," Tate said. "How's that going?"

"Five couples for four weekly nights of baking fun," Mel said. "Other than the Bickersons, it's going well."

"Bickersons?" he asked.

"That's what we call the Bakersons," Angie said. "Neither one of them knows a pastry bag from a garbage bag but they'll fight to the death about it."

"Some couples are like that," Tate said.

Angie fished the keys to the shop out of her purse and led the way into the bakery, after deactivating the alarm.

Mel glanced at Tate out of the corner of her eye as she followed him into the shop. It had been three months since his fiancée had been murdered and even though he had been duped into getting engaged to her (she drugged him and then pretended he proposed), Mel wondered if the upcoming lovers' holiday was making him wistful.

"Thank God I don't have to buy anyone flowers or candy or even a card," he said. He shuddered in his charcoal gray power suit. Well, that answered that.

Angie glanced at him with a small smile. " 'Hearts will be practical only when they are made unbreakable.' "

"*The Wizard of Oz.*" Tate identified the quote. "Nice."

Angie bowed her head in acknowledgment before flicking on the overhead lights.

The three of them had met when they were in junior high school. A mutual love of old movies and junk food had sealed their friendship, which was now going on twenty years. They still spent almost every weekend together watching old movies and now liked to quote them to one another and see if they could stump one another.

"For the record, my heart is not broken," he protested. "Merely dented."

Angie grinned at him and Mel felt an anxious butterfly flap its wings down in her belly. How could Tate not see that when Angie smiled at him her heart was in her eyes? She literally lit up from the inside. A beautiful girl to begin with, when she looked at Tate, she was breathtaking.

Mel was torn between wanting to smack Tate into getting a clue and keeping him ignorant for the sake of their friendship. After all, what if Angie and Tate did get together? She'd be shut out. It was completely selfish, but she wasn't sure if she was ready for that.

Tate pushed back his starched cuff and checked his snazzy Omega. "Gotta go. Big meeting with the shareholders. Call me if the giant cupcake causes any more trouble."

"Will do," Mel and Angie answered together.

Tate hugged each of them in turn and then left. The bells on the door handle jangled in his wake.

Mel and Angie exchanged a look, and Angie shook her head. "No, I'm not going to tell him how I feel."

"But . . ."

"Change of subject please," Angie said as she pushed through the swinging door into the kitchen beyond. "Like, when are you and Joe going to seal the deal?"

Mel followed her. "What makes you think we haven't?"

"Oh, please, if you and Joe had slept together, I'd know," she said.

Mel couldn't argue the point, well, she could but it would be futile. Angie had known her forever and Joe was Angie's older brother, one of her seven older brothers, so she'd known him even longer. There was no hiding from Angie.

Mel had lusted for Joe DeLaura from the first time she clapped eyes on him when she was twelve years old. And now, they were actually dating. Sometimes she had to pinch herself to believe it. But then, when she remembered they hadn't progressed much past hand-holding, she began to fret.

"Change of subject," she said.

Angie gave her a knowing nod. "Fine. What are we cooking tonight?"

"Kiss Me Cupcakes."

"Describe please."

Angie dropped her purse on the steel table and headed straight for the coffeepot. Mel talked while Angie started a fresh pot.

"Chocolate mint chip cupcake with red and white swirled mint icing and a big Hershey Kiss planted in the middle."

"Wrapper on or off?"

"On," Mel said. "I like the silver foil as a decoration."

"Do I need to run to Smart and Final for any supplies?" Angie asked.

Mel checked the stock in the large plastic bins they kept along one wall of the shop. Flour, check. Sugar, check. Baking soda, check. Then she poked her head in the large walk-in refrigerator. Butter, check. Eggs, check. And lastly, she looked in the pantry for the lesser used items. Chocolate, in various shapes and sizes, check.

"No, I think we're good," she said. "I'm going to go grab a shower. Give me fifteen and we can get started."

"Sounds good," Angie said. "You do realize, though, that Olivia has issued a challenge that can't be ignored."

"Don't you worry," Mel said. "It won't be. I promise."